LOVE THY NEIGHBOR

"You've spoiled me," Quintin crooned, smiling down on Victoria's upturned face.

Victoria's gaze caressed his features, lingering on the sweeping arch of his thick black eyebrows, the tiny lines around his laughing eyes, and the sensual curve of his masculine mouth.

"I'm considering unspoiling you," she teased.

"Too late." His head lowered and he nuzzled her neck.

"I'll move away."

"I'll follow you, Vicky. I'll sail the world searching for you."

Victoria melted against his body, luxuriating in the unyielding strength that was Quintin Lord's, her arms going around his slim waist. Closing her eyes, she gave in to the powerful passions coursing through her as Quintin sculpted her body with his fingers. He was the artist, the sculptor molding and shaping her to his will.

"I need you, Vicky," he murmured against her ear.

She stiffened. She didn't want him to need her; she wanted him to want her. "Let me go, Quintin."

He released her, staring. What had he done? She silently made her way out of the kitchen.

Had he moved too quickly? He had to remind himself that Victoria Jones was different. He couldn't rush her.

A wry smile curved his mouth. He would wait her out. She wasn't going anywhere and neither was he.

HOME *Sweet* HOME

Rochelle Alers

PINNACLE BOOKS
KENSINGTON PUBLISHING CORP.

PINNACLE BOOKS are published by

Kensington Publishing Corp.
850 Third Avenue
New York, NY 10022

First Pinnacle Books Printing: June, 1996

Printed in the United States of America

10 9 8 7 6 5 4 3 2 1

To Elizabeth Bailey Liebscher—
for true friendship,

Jo-Ann Leitner—
the inspiration for Jo,

and Frances Lavelle—
for all the laughs!

If you and your neighbor have a difference of opinion, settle it between yourselves and do not reveal any secrets.

—Proverbs 25:9

One

The large airy kitchen was the most functional room in Victoria Jones's newly purchased condominium apartment. A contractor had installed an additional microwave oven, two built-in, eye-level industrial ovens, a rotisserie, an eight-burner gas range with a grill and exhaust system, and a commercial walk-in refrigerator and freezer. These appliances were tools of her trade, and now she was ready to operate VJ Catering at its new location.

Baltimore, Maryland, was not very far from Washington, D.C., yet it was far enough away for her to begin a new life.

Baltimore was far enough away from Victoria's parents, who lamented relentlessly that it was time she consider remarrying.

It was far enough away from her friends, who had settled into a comfortable routine of coming home to a husband and children.

It was also far enough away from her ex-husband, his new wife, and their children. Children could have been born to her and Richard if she had been able to conceive again.

But none of that mattered any longer. She had begun anew—with a new home and a new enterprising business.

She walked up two steps from the brick-walled kitchen to the expanse of the living and dining areas and up the curving staircase, with its decorative wrought-iron railing.

At the top was a loft containing three bedrooms with Palladian windows and towering sloped ceilings.

Everywhere she turned in the apartment there was a sense of space and light.

How different, Victoria thought, this home was from the one she had abandoned when her marriage ended. She and Richard had lived in a stately English Tudor structure with dark walls, floors, and darkly colored leaded windows.

Elegance and tradition. That was what she and Richard Morgan exemplified as young Washingtonians. They were heirs to a dynasty, a dynasty of elite African-Americans who were as much a part of the Capital District's history as was the Washington Monument.

Pulling back her shoulders, Victoria sucked in her breath and exhaled slowly. It had been a while since she had thought about Richard, and thinking about him always brought pain. Somehow it was impossible to remember the good times they had once shared. She decided to exorcise Richard from her mind with the thing he detested most. Her dancing.

Climbing the staircase with a fluidity and grace that had come from a lifetime of classical dance training, she walked into the smaller bedroom she had designed as a dance studio.

Her reflection stared back at her from a wall of mirrored glass. Thick, chemically straightened hair was brushed back off her forehead to the nape of her neck. At thirty-one, she was five foot three, but a long and graceful neck and an incredibly slender body made her appear taller and much younger.

Dressed in a white leotard, matching footless tights, and faded pink ballet slippers, she moved over to the barre and began a series of stretching techniques. She no longer danced professionally, but years of training could not be erased even after the shattered bones in her right ankle.

The orthopedic surgeon's prediction of a speedy recovery was realized but his conclusion that the ankle would never be strong enough to withstand the hours of practice demanded from a professional dancer also bore truth.

At twenty-one, a poorly executed *entrechat quartre* had cost Victoria Morgan a dance career, a tiny life nestled in her womb, and two years later, her marriage.

This morning she executed *pliés, jetés,* and several arabesques with relative ease. Forty minutes later the routine concluded with a perfect *tour en l'air*—one complete turn of her body and a graceful *révérence.* A satisfied smile touched her expressive full lips as silent applause roared its approval. She had given a flawless performance.

Her workout ended, as it did every morning, with a luxuriating shower and her velvety-soft skin glowing with a scented cream cologne of pungent flowers and woodsy oils. She slipped into a pair of ivory satin-and-lace bikini underpants and a matching demi-bra. Her hands faltered as her mind registered a low thumping sound reverberating off the bedroom walls.

It was music. There was no mistaking the deep moan of an organ, but it was the accompanying male voice singing a soulful ballad that transfixed Victoria. Whoever was playing the music had turned up the volume.

Throwing a tropical floral print kimono over her half-nude body, she raced out of the bedroom and down the staircase.

The sound of the music grew louder and louder until Victoria felt the pulsating bass in her chest. The only time she had known music to be as loud was when she attended concerts or dance clubs.

Flinging open the front door, she was met with the full force of the powerful sound. The door to the neighboring apartment stood open. There was no doubt her neighbor enjoyed his or her music—at full tilt.

She had closed on the purchase of the apartment more

than three months before, but it had taken that long to renovate it before moving in, and she still had not met her neighbor on the two blocks of five row houses, each containing two duplex units.

Most of the units were purchased by young professionals under forty, the remaining to retired couples who no longer had to mow lawns, rake leaves, or shovel snow the occasional time it fell. However, it appeared as if her closest neighbor's development had been arrested at adolescence or the person had undergone some degree of hearing loss.

Victoria walked into her neighbor's entryway and froze. The sight that greeted her was a shock. The sound of the raucous music paled as she noted bundles of old newspapers, palettes of dried paints, and stacks of stretched canvases against every inch of wall space in both the living and dining rooms, discarded articles of intimate apparel—male and female—crushed pizza and take-out food cartons, fishing gear, and a large schnauzer, whose hot breath washed over her bare thighs.

The dog's luminous eyes were partially concealed under a fringe of shaggy black hair as it peered up at her. Victoria prayed the dog wasn't vicious. In any case, she did not want to make any sudden motion that would startle it.

Swallowing painfully, she managed a hoarse, "Nice dog." Her words were drowned out by the rhythmic pounding of the music.

The animal reacted to her friendly greeting by rising on its hind legs and resting both front paws on her shoulders. The weight of the powerful dog knocked her backward and she lost her balance, falling down onto a pile of soiled laundry. She struggled vainly to free herself from the tangle of clothes and the dog sitting comfortably on her middle.

"Let her up, Hannibal!"

It took several seconds before she registered the sound

of the male voice. The command was soft, yet carried a ring of unyielding authority.

The man had not *shouted* at the dog because the music had stopped. She had been too startled by the scene she had come upon to realize the absence of the driving, pumping rhythm.

"Hannibal!"

As the dog obediently moved off her body, Victoria stared up at the tall figure looming above her. The man extended a hand and she grasped it. In one smooth, strong motion she was standing. Clear brown eyes in a bearded brown face the color of burnished oak narrowed in concentration. The direction of the man's gaze was fixed on a spot below her neck.

Glancing down, Victoria discovered her wrap hung open, permitting her rescuer a full view of her body in her skimpy undergarments.

With as much aplomb as she could manage, she retied the sash to the kimono. Tilting her chin, she frowned up at the man.

"Do you mind not playing your music so loud," she said haughtily.

"I like it loud," he retorted, a small smile softening his mouth.

She felt her temper flare. "Look, Mr. . . ."

"Lord," he supplied. "Quintin Lord." Grinning, he gestured toward the dog standing at his side. "Of course you've met Hannibal," he continued smoothly. "Hannibal's usually not so demonstrative with his affection. But being a male he just couldn't resist getting close to a beautiful woman."

Gritting her teeth, she warned, "Please keep the music down."

If possible, Quintin's smile widened, displaying a mouth filled with large white teeth. "I'm somewhat partial to Victoria's Secret myself," he remarked, lifting an eyebrow.

At first she thought he was asking her name, but then realized he was referring to her lingerie. Turning on her heel, she stalked out of his apartment and back into her own. She closed the door with a resounding slam but not before she heard a loud chuckle from Quintin Lord.

Victoria stood with her back against the door, trying to regain control of her temper. *He's rude . . . and he's a pig,* she thought. A pig who lives in a pigsty. And his dog was also rude. If she hadn't fallen on the pile of dirty clothes she could have broken her neck.

She made her way to the living room and flopped down on an oyster-white armchair with a matching ottoman. A moan escaped her. Quintin Lord had turned on his music again. The only consolation was that it wasn't as loud as it had been before.

Two

Quintin pushed the litter strewn about the living room into large green plastic bags. The two weeks away had dulled his memory. His last assignment must have left him more stressed out and dazed than usual. He made it a practice not to clean up until he completed a project, and, as evidenced by the number of take-out food containers he had gone through while doing the graphics for an ad agency pitching a new line of beauty products, the normal clutter now bordered on slovenliness. After he had completed the ads he promptly packed enough supplies to spend the next two weeks on his boat visiting the Florida Keys and several Caribbean islands.

Picking up a lacy bra, Quintin dangled it from a forefinger. Of all of the models he photographed, Alicia was the one who always seemed to leave an article of clothing behind. Smiling, he wondered if she ever ran out of underwear. The bra went into the plastic bag with the other discarded trash.

Thinking of underwear reminded Quintin of his new neighbor. The delicate white lacy triangles against her sienna-brown body had been a definite turn-on. He had painted and photographed more nude and near-nude women than he could count since becoming an artist. A woman's bare breasts, thigh, or derriere held as much excitement for Quintin Lord as a speck of lint on his camera lens.

But the beautiful woman with the perfect body who had moved in next door was different, very different.

Her face was small—oval—and her features were even. Everything about her was young and fresh—except for her eyes. They were large and haunted; seemingly haunted with a sadness that belied her young years.

Quintin picked up a windbreaker and tossed it onto a pile of soiled clothing. The motion forced the large schnauzer to move to another comfortable location. Visibly disturbed, the dog growled deep in his throat.

"Don't get too relaxed, Hannibal," he warned his pet. "I have to go to the supermarket and *you* have a date to be groomed." Hannibal growled again, burying his muzzle in the clothes.

Quintin shot Hannibal a look of indifference. "It doesn't matter to me, sport. I can always order take-out." Hannibal only ate canned dog food.

Hannibal rose to his feet, large black eyes trained on his master. To Quintin it seemed as if he and Hannibal were telepathically connected. The dog always sensed Quintin's mercurial moods, while he controlled Hannibal with a mere glance or hand signal; the two had been inseparable since he bought the puppy from his dog-breeder sister two years ago.

"I thought you'd see it my way," Quintin remarked, smiling.

He put out several bags of garbage for the day's pickup, then gathered the soiled clothing that had accumulated from the two-week sailing excursion, while Hannibal waited patiently.

The animal's short tail twitched in excitement as he led him out of the apartment to the four-wheeler parked in one of the garages at the rear of the row houses.

The late-spring sun was unusually warm and foretold of a characteristically hot summer. Quintin enjoyed the change of seasons, but found a special peace sailing miles from land, having only water, sky, and the feel of a deck, rising and falling, under his feet.

His next assignment was to create a series of ads for an African-American clothing designer whose popularity had come from her use of Moroccan beads, Ghanaian cloth wraparound skirts, and Kente cloth trimmings. He predicted the assignment would take three weeks, at the end of which time he would again feel the sensual roll of *Jamila*'s smooth deck under his feet for several weeks before again accepting a new commission.

Quintin made several stops, dropping off laundry before he deposited Hannibal at the dog grooming salon. There was an hour's wait before Hannibal would be ready, so he decided to have his own hair and a month's growth of whiskers cut at the unisex salon located in the minimall. What he enjoyed most about living in the Baltimore suburb was having every big-city convenience on a small-town scale.

Thirty minutes later, his close-cropped hair soft and shining from a shampoo and conditioner, and his brown jaw smooth from an expert shave, Quintin walked into a spacious air-cooled supermarket.

Seeing to his personal needs had always given him a sense of independence, and at thirty-seven he had no immediate plan to alter his lifestyle or change his bachelor status. All he needed was his work, his boat, and his dog to feel complete; as the fifth child in a family of six boys and three girls, he had been forced to carve out his own space and establish his importance and independence early within the Lord household.

He strolled up and down wide aisles, selecting cans and packages, tossing them aimlessly into his shopping cart. He turned into the dairy aisle and saw her.

His gaze moved slowly and sensuously over the curve

of her hips in the slim black denim skirt she had paired with a white T-shirt. Her shapely legs were bare and her tiny feet were encased in black leather flats.

Quintin felt the heat rush through his own body, recalling the woman's near-nude body earlier that morning.

Victoria glanced up and found a man staring at her. There was something vaguely familiar about him, but she could not place his face.

The man was tall, nearly six foot, and arrogantly handsome. His golden-brown face was deeply tanned, his hair cut close and brushed back off a high, wide forehead. A thick mustache obscured his upper lip while failing to hide the sensual fullness of his lower one. He smiled, and recognition dawned. He was her neighbor Quintin Lord!

Victoria chided herself for not recognizing him. There weren't too many men bold or secure enough to wear small gold hoops in *both* ears.

She shivered, not wanting to acknowledge the chill pervading her limbs was from Quintin Lord's penetrating gaze, but was the result instead of the cold air emanating from the freezer cases.

"Good afternoon, Mr. Lord," Victoria said with a deadly calm she did not feel as she perused the crisp khaki shirt he wore with matching slacks and tan deck shoes.

Quintin inclined his head, smiling. "Good afternoon, neighbor."

Victoria extended a small hand. "Victoria Jones."

He had unwittingly guessed her first name. He considered that a good omen.

He flashed a disarming smile, grasping her hand. "I'm sorry we got off to a bad start this morning. Please accept my apology."

She extracted her fingers from his warm grip, returning the smile. "Apology graciously accepted."

He peered into her overflowing shopping cart. "You must have quite an appetite."

Victoria laughed, the sound light and carefree. When her eyes crinkled, her gentle and delicate beauty hit Quintin full force.

"I'm having a housewarming celebration Saturday afternoon," she explained.

At least she hadn't said *we're* having a housewarming, he thought, ruling out a roommate or live-in lover.

Quintin continued to stare at Victoria, his eyes photographing her face and committing everything about it to memory. He had photographed and painted women much more beautiful than Victoria Jones yet there was something about her that haunted him, drew him to her against his will.

He glanced at his watch, then at the contents of his own shopping cart. He still had a few more items to select before picking up Hannibal.

"I'll let you finish up your shopping," he said to Victoria. "See you around."

Victoria nodded. "See you around," she repeated.

She watched Quintin as he moved down the aisle, admiring how well he wore his clothes. His apartment may have been a disaster but Quintin Lord's attire was clean and neat.

Victoria turned her attention back to the long list of items she had to purchase for the housewarming event only two days away. She was looking forward to having her friends over to her new apartment with an almost childlike excitement. It was to be the first time in a long time that the printed invitation read Victoria Jones and not Richard and Victoria Morgan.

She selected her dairy items before heading over to the produce section. Summer fruits were in season and she picked out the most appealing strawberries, blueberries, cantaloupe, several other types of melons, and a variety of fresh vegetables.

She completed her shopping and merely raised an eyebrow when the cashier totaled her purchases. As she handed the cashier three large bills, the bagger quickly and expertly packed her groceries. She thanked the clerk, then pushed her cart through the sliding doors and out into the early-afternoon sunshine.

A tall male figure moved beside her, grasping the handle to the cart. Victoria's short gasp of surprise was momentary. She glanced up at the smiling face of Quintin Lord.

"I thought you'd need help trying to fit everything in your car," he explained quietly.

She stared at the thick brush of hair covering his upper lip before her gaze moved to his strong neck.

"It'll all fit," she said, raising her gaze to meet his. "I have a minivan."

She had bought the vehicle when she'd started her catering business. There was no way she would be able to transport trays of food and serving pieces, stacks of linen, serving tables, and an occasional hired server in an ordinary car.

Quintin steered the cart out to the parking lot. "Then I'll help you load it," he said in a firm tone. "Where are you parked?"

Victoria quickened her pace to keep up with his long strides. "That's not necessary."

Quintin ignored her protest. "Where's your van?"

She knew it was useless to argue with him as she pointed to her right. "It's the navy-blue one in the first row."

She followed Quintin, opening the sliding side door and watching as he emptied the cart, stacking the many brown paper bags in the cargo area and on the fold-down rear seat.

Victoria noted the smooth ripple of firm muscle under the dark-brown flesh of his arms uncovered by the turned-back cuffs to his khaki shirt. She was fascinated by the fluid, graceful line of Quintin's body as he reached for, picked up, and put down each bag. Despite his height, she mused, Quintin Lord easily could have been a dancer.

Quintin pushed the empty cart into a line with others, then turned back to Victoria. He had felt her watching him, and he wondered what was going on behind her haunted gaze.

"I've performed my good deed for today. I do hope that I'm *truly* forgiven," he said, his eyes crinkling attractively as he displayed his winning smile.

She arched a curving eyebrow. "For what?"

"For my inappropriate remark about your undergarments."

Victoria remembered his comment about her skimpy lingerie and a wave of heat flared in her cheeks. It was not his fault that she had been so scantily clad. And if she had not been so unnerved by the ear-shattering volume of his music she never would have walked into his apartment half dressed.

"Yes, Quintin. You're *truly* forgiven," she returned with a soft laugh.

Quintin leaned closer, the heat from his breath and body increasing the warmth in Victoria's. "See you around, neighbor."

Quintin's *see around,* the small gold hoops in each ear, the thick brush of his silky mustache, and the graceful leanness of his lithe body nagged at Victoria on her drive home.

Something about Quintin Lord signaled a primitive warning for her to stay away from this very attractive male.

I hope he's married or he at least has a steady girlfriend, she thought, remembering the feminine underwear tossed recklessly on his living-room floor. That would serve as an excuse and a healthy reminder to keep Quintin

Lord at a comfortable distance, for she could not permit herself to get close to a man again.

She had given Richard her love, her body, and her life, and it still had not been enough for him.

Victoria stared at the traffic light in the intersection, then glanced over to her left. Sitting in a four-wheeler waiting for the light to change was Quintin Lord. She studied his profile and turned away, pulling out into traffic as soon as the light changed from red to green.

She was too far away to see Quintin's expression in her rearview mirror. If she had, she would have been unnerved. But more than that she would have been shocked if she had known his thoughts.

Three

"Do you like her, Hannibal?" Quintin asked his lounging pet.

The dog raised his head, focused soulful eyes on his master, then lowered his shaggy head back to his front paws.

"What is it about her—this Vicky Jones—that's different?" Quintin questioned in his monologue with Hannibal. She's perfect, he thought. Victoria Jones was not classically beautiful, but she was perfect. He wanted to photograph her; he wanted a likeness of his diminutive neighbor for himself for an eternity.

As a skillfully trained commercial artist, Quintin knew what to look for whenever he photographed a subject: the right camera angle, the proper lighting—and the most effective ways to bring out the best in a subject without artificial props or retouching. This inherent skill made him tops in his field and highly sought after. He was discriminating in whom he accepted as a client, earning fees and commissions that far exceeded those of his colleagues while permitting him to act out his fantasies.

Sailing had been a boyhood craving. After he had worked enough years to save sufficient money, he had a boat built to his specifications. Now, at thirty-seven he discovered he had another craving—Victoria Jones. Without rhyme or reason he wanted the woman.

"Perhaps I'm going through a midlife crisis," Quintin

continued to a silent Hannibal. Hannibal blinked slowly at Quintin with mysterious dark eyes.

"Hell, I'm too young for a midlife crisis!" Quintin sputtered. He flopped down to an armchair after pushing a stack of magazines onto the floor. Lacing his fingers together, he steepled his forefingers and brought them to his mustached upper lip. The two fingers stroked the thick coarse hair in an up-and-down motion.

He wanted Victoria Jones. He wanted to know her in every way possible. A part of his body stirred and he knew he wanted to know her in the most intimate way possible.

Quintin buried his face in his hands. He *was* going through a midlife crisis. It had been too long since he had lusted after a woman—any woman.

His sex drive was as healthy as any normal man's, but recently he hadn't felt driven to sleep with any particular woman.

He had proven to himself that he did not need sexual intercourse to exist.

No, he didn't need any woman to exist—that's what he'd always told himself—but some foreign, hidden emotion taunted him now, telling him that was not the case. Why hadn't he felt this way before meeting Victoria Jones?

Victoria felt a strange presence and she turned slowly. Standing outside of her kitchen was Quintin Lord's giant schnauzer.

The dog stood motionless, blinking at her through a fringe of shaggy hair. His tightly curling black coat had been stripped until the pale pink of his flesh was visible.

Crossing her arms under her breasts, Victoria smiled at Hannibal. "Just because I left my door open, that didn't mean you could walk in without an invitation."

The dog lowered its head and turned to walk away. "No!" she cried out. "You don't have to go." Much to her surprise, Hannibal turned and flopped down to the cool wood floor. Resting his muzzle on his front paws, he closed his eyes and began snoring.

"Well, I'll be," she whispered softly, wondering if Quintin knew the whereabouts of his pet. She realized he knew the dog could not have gone very far. The front door of the condominium was self-locking and she was certain only she and Quintin occupied the two duplex apartments.

Victoria busied herself putting away her groceries. The smell of wood still lingered in the spacious kitchen from newly hung oak cabinets. She rinsed fruits and vegetables before storing them away in the bins in the commercial refrigerator, mentally outlining her menu for the housewarming celebration. The dishes she planned to serve would demonstrate her expertise in the culinary arts. The Saturday gathering would be all the advertising she would need to start up her business.

The position of the sun's rays slanting through the kitchen's skylight shifted and Victoria glanced up at the clock over the sink. It was too late for lunch, so she decided on an early dinner.

Hannibal forgotten, Victoria washed, sliced, and set aside several boned chicken breasts. Quickly and expertly she counted out a generous portion of snow peas, then sliced a large carrot, yellow and red bell peppers, a celery stalk, and fresh shiitake mushrooms on a cutting board countertop. She added minced garlic and fresh ginger to a bowl of Oriental sesame oil and soy sauce, then ground fresh cilantro and shallots in a food processor, adding them to the marinade along with lemon juice, freshly ground pepper, and salt. She poured the mixture over the chicken, which would be ready for grilling within the hour.

Stepping over Hannibal, Victoria went upstairs to change her clothes. Slipping out of her skirt, she pulled on a pair of white loose-fitting Indian cotton slacks with a drawstring waist.

Minutes later she returned to the living room and put several CDs on a carousel. The apartment was flooded with the sensual voice of Luther Vandross.

Victoria's romantic mood was mirrored by the musical selections she had chosen: Vandross, Anita Baker, Brenda Russell, and David Sanborn. If she had felt stressful, her choices would have been different: Yanni, Andreas Volleneider, or David Arkenstone. New Age music melted away her anxiety, transporting her to a sphere of fantasy.

It had been three years since she had been swept away by fantasy. At twenty-eight, she met a young man in France. They both had enrolled in a ten-week graduate culinary program at the La Varenne École de Cuisine, completing their courses successfully; however, their liaison did not survive the predictable summer romance syndrome.

Victoria had no desire to marry Masud and set up an eating establishment in his native Burundi. It also had not mattered to her that Masud was a true prince, the eldest son of a tribal chief, heir to both his father's throne and his millions. Prince Masud was quick to explain that his family owned the largest coffee plantation in the small, densely populated, land-locked African country.

She saw Masud off at Orly Airport, telling him she would always think of him as a special friend. Masud bowed over her hand and called her his queen.

She left Paris a week later and returned to the United States as a highly trained and skilled banquet and pastry chef. She spent another two years working for a prestigious Washington, D.C., hotel before deciding it was time she went into business for herself.

Returning to the kitchen, she looked around for Hannibal, searching the pantry, dining area, and the entryway. Shrugging her shoulders, she closed the door. The dog had probably gone back home.

Victoria completed the preparations for her dinner, making a Greek salad to accompany her main dish of grilled chicken with stir-fry vegetables. She busied herself for the next hour while the chicken absorbed the mixture, then, switching on the grill, she placed several strips on the red-hot grating, turning them quickly to prevent overcooking . . .

Victoria heard the soft chiming of her doorbell and went still. She made her way to the door and peered through the peephole. Recognizing Quintin Lord, she opened the door. Her pulse leaped as she surveyed his lithe form in a pair of paint-spattered shorts and an equally paint-spattered tank top.

"Yes?" Her voice was lower and more husky than normal, and for the first time Quintin noticed her distinctive southern drawl.

His gaze swept quickly over her face. "I'm looking for Hannibal. Have you seen him?"

Victoria opened the door wider. "He was here, but I can't find him now. I thought he had gone home."

Quintin shifted a black eyebrow, his gaze locked with Victoria's. "Do you mind if I try calling him?"

She stepped back, and Quintin walked into the entryway. Placing both forefingers in his mouth, he whistled shrilly. Seconds later Hannibal bounded down the stairs, tail twitching nervously. He jumped up and down against Quintin's thigh, excited to be reunited with his master.

Quintin scratched Hannibal behind his ears. "Hey, homey. What are you doing hiding out here?"

Hannibal responded by barking loudly and winding his way in and out between Quintin's legs.

Victoria laughed as she watched the dog's antics. It was apparent Hannibal was glad to see Quintin. Her smile faded slowly. As much as she did not want to admit it, she was also glad to see him. In his revealing outfit his sun-darkened body was exquisite.

She suddenly gasped loudly. "Oh, no!" Her food was burning. Turning, she left Quintin staring at her retreating back as she raced into the kitchen.

She managed to salvage several strips of grilled chicken before they were charred beyond recognition.

"It smells wonderful," Quintin remarked, leaning against the entrance to the kitchen. He had followed her. His sherry-colored gaze swept over the furnishings in the large space. "And it looks as if you're ready to do some serious cooking in here," he added softly.

"I'm a caterer," she admitted, placing several more strips of chicken on the grill.

Quintin walked into the kitchen, carefully noting the ovens, commercial refrigerator and freezer, and the strange-looking utensils and culinary gadgets suspended from overhead hooks.

Resting a hip against a counter, he stared at Victoria's delicate profile as she concentrated on the grill. "What's your specialty?"

She smiled at him. "Everything. I'm a master chef."

"What did you have to do to become a master chef?"

"Demonstrate skills of an exceptional level in cooking, baking, presentation, cold foods, nutrition, and facility design." She sounded like an culinary school advertisement.

Quintin's impassive expression did not change. He never would have guessed her profession. He figured her for someone who worked with small children.

He took a seat on a tall stool near the cooking island, watching Victoria examine the strips of chicken.

"Was it difficult?" he asked without warning.

She turned slowly, taking her time in answering his query with one of her own. "Was what difficult?"

"Venturing into a field that has been dominated by men."

"I never let that deter me," she answered as honestly as she could. There were times when she met some opposition, but refused to let it thwart her goal to become a master chef.

Quintin leaned back, resting both arms on the back of the stool. The motion caused the cotton fabric of his tank top to stretch across the expanse of his broad chest.

The sensual, unconscious motion was not lost on Victoria as she averted her gaze from his body. Quintin Lord was slim and loose-limbed, yet solid and muscled. It was evident he worked out regularly.

"Did you always want to become a chef?" he continued with his questioning.

Victoria shook her head, not looking at him. "No." She swallowed the rising lump in her throat. It was never easy to talk about her aborted dance career. It brought back too many other unpleasant memories.

"I was trained to be a dancer," she admitted.

Quintin gave her body a long, penetrating look. He glanced down at her tiny feet in a pair of white ballet slippers. Victoria felt her cheeks heat up as his gaze retraced its path, then lingered on her face.

"What kind of painting do you do?" she asked, giving him an equally bold stare.

She had to admit to herself that he was the most attractive man she had seen in a long time. There was something lazily seductive about his lounging stance. Her gaze moved to his mustached mouth and she wondered what it would be like to feel the hair on his upper lip against her own mouth. Would it tickle? Would it scratch? Or would it feel both rough and soothing at the same time?

"I'm a freelance commercial artist."

"Are you good?" she questioned quietly.

His eyes darkened with an emotion that seemed to drink

in everything about her. "Yes, Vicky Jones," he replied just as softly. "I'm good. In fact, I'm very, very good."

She smiled, unaware of the captivating picture she presented. "I'm glad to know that," she replied, knowing he wasn't talking solely about his artistic ability.

"What medium do you work in?" she questioned.

"Primarily oil, acrylic, watercolors, and on rare occasions charcoal. Why do you ask?"

"I'm looking for several watercolors for my living room. I've gone to a few shops and galleries, but I haven't found anything I'd like to look at day after day."

Quintin moved off the stool and stared down at her upturned face. The haunted look in her eyes was absent and in its place was openness and curiosity.

"I may have a few watercolors tucked away at my place. I'll try to hunt them up, then offer you a private showing."

Victoria sensed his teasing mood. "Are you serving hors d'oeuvres and champagne?"

He leaned closer, grinning broadly. "I'll supply the artwork and champagne. The only hors d'oeuvres I'd be able to offer would be chicken fingers with a plethora of plastic-packaged sauces. I'm willing to wager I have the most extensive collection of take-out menus of anyone within a three-mile radius."

Victoria laughed. "I'll supply the hors d'oeuvres."

Quintin grasped her right hand, pressing his lips to her soft palm. "Bless you, child."

She almost gasped aloud at the pleasurable jolt racing up and down her arm. The feel of the thick brush of hair on her sensitive flesh was intoxicating. She stared at his lowered head, unable to believe this man, her neighbor, could turn her on so easily.

"What time, Quintin?"

He raised his head, still holding on to her hand. His brow furrowed. "What?"

"What time do you want to show me your paintings?"

Quintin released her hand. Touching Victoria Jones and inhaling her feminine fragrance had unnerved him. "Seven," he said quickly.

"A.M. or P.M.?"

Regaining control of his emotions, he crossed his arms over his chest. "I jog at seven A.M. You're more than welcome to join me."

Victoria shook her head. "I don't jog. I broke my ankle ten years ago, and there are times when I can't put too much pressure on it."

"Are you all right walking?"

She nodded.

"Then we can walk tomorrow."

"Perhaps some other time," she suggested, tactfully turning down his invitation. Agreeing to see him to purchase artwork was one thing. Going for early-morning walks was something else entirely different.

"Then it'll be seven P.M.," Quintin countered. "My place or yours?" he asked with a wide grin.

Victoria remembered the clutter in Quintin's apartment. "My place—if that's okay with you."

"Your place it is. See you around."

Turning on his heel, Quintin turned to leave, whistling softly. Hannibal's head came up alertly and he pranced after his master.

Victoria followed after a few minutes and locked the door. She retreated to the kitchen, humming along with Luther Vandross's "Superstar," ignoring the little voice warning her to stay away from Quintin Lord.

It's not going to be that easy, she thought. After all, the man was her neighbor. There was no way she could avoid him even if she wanted to.

But she had to admit to herself that she didn't want to. Not yet.

Four

Victoria glanced around her living room, pleased at what she saw. Soft light from a floor lamp bathed everything in a warm pink glow. A sofa, love seat, and matching armchair in an oyster-white Haitian cotton cradled watered silk throw pillows in mauve and gray and complemented the pale-pink area rug on the highly polished wood floor.

The mouth-watering aromas from her day-long marathon cooking session had been extinguished by the highly efficient exhaust system, and newly opening pink-and-white tulips in a large vase filled the room with their fragrance.

She let out a soft sigh of relief. She had prepared all of the dishes she would need for her Saturday housewarming celebration: hors d'oeuvres, main and accompanying side dishes, and delectable desserts. The only dishes she hadn't prepared and refrigerated were the fresh green salads.

Lighting fat white vanilla-scented candles on the cherrywood side tables, she stood back and admired her handiwork. The dining-room table had been set with a snowy linen cloth with elaborate cutout designs, translucent china, gleaming silver, and delicate crystal stemware.

Positioning a fork, Victoria examined it for even a dot of tarnish. Satisfied that everything was in order, she picked up a remote device and flicked on her stereo unit.

The ballet score from Aaron Copland's *Billy the Kid* flowed from the speakers. She had danced the Americana ballet at fourteen, and along with *Swan Lake* and the *Nutcracker* it had immediately become one of her favorites.

When the doorbell chimed, Victoria glanced at the clock on the mantel over the living-room fireplace. It was exactly seven. *He's on time,* she thought, making her way to the door.

When she opened the door, Quintin's easy smile was slow in coming. He found it hard to believe the subtle change in Victoria's appearance could transform her ethereal femininity into one that virtually shouted its presence with the softly curling hair framing her face, the light cover of makeup highlighting her features, the shimmering white silk blouse and slacks covering her body, and the exotic scents clinging to her warm brown flesh.

His smile broadened and Victoria stepped aside. "Please come in," she urged, taking the bottle of champagne he offered her. "I'll put this in some ice."

He followed her into the dining room, admiring the soft shadows of the pink light reflecting off the pale walls.

Victoria settled the bottle of champagne in a large crystal bowl filled with ice, watching Quintin as he moved into the living room. He examined the photographs of her family on the mantel while she silently admired the graceful slimness of his male body in his black shirt and slacks.

He turned without warning and caught her intense stare. Victoria felt heat steal into her cheeks, but she did not drop her gaze. She pushed her hands into the hidden pockets of her slacks to hide the slight trembling of them.

He returned her bold stare, seemingly reaching into her very thoughts. He saw curiosity and some other emotion he could not yet define.

"Lovely," he said in a quiet tone. "You and your home," he explained when she shifted her eyebrows.

"Would you like a tour while the champagne chills?"

Quintin moved closer to her, pulling her left hand from the pocket of her slacks. He cradled her much smaller hand in his, squeezing her fingers gently. "Lead on."

Victoria registered the heat and strength of his strong grip and threaded her fingers through his. She smiled up at him. "We'll begin with the second level."

Hand-in-hand Victoria led Quintin in and out of the three rooms. He chuckled softly when he saw the room she had set up as her dance studio.

"Do you ever give private performances?" he teased.

She flicked off the light, shaking her head. "No."

"Not even by special request?" he insisted, standing very close to her.

"No!"

Victoria could have bitten off her tongue. She had not meant to snap at him, but she would never dance for an audience again. She would dance for one person—herself.

Quintin watched a myriad of emotions cross her face. "Was it that painful, Vicky?"

"The injury or my giving up a dance career?" She answered his question with one of her own. She did not add giving up a child she would never hold or a husband she had loved unselfishly.

"Everything. Everything that went along with giving up your dance career."

She managed a brave smile. "It was painful, but I recovered."

Quintin moved closer, trapping her body between his and the door. "I take that to mean that you're carrying no excess baggage from your past."

Victoria felt somewhat annoyed by his line of questioning. He was asking a lot from her. After all, he was only her neighbor—and a stranger at that.

Tilting her chin, she stared up into his sherry-colored eyes. "What you see is what you get," she answered in a flippant tone.

He flashed a devilish grin, his teeth showing whitely under the thick mustache. "And just what is it you're offering, Miss Jones?"

"What any other neighbor would offer, Mr. Lord. A cup of sugar, picking up your newspaper or mail when you're on vacation, and perhaps bringing you a cup of hot tea if you're down with the flu."

He stepped back, surprise clearly written on his face. "Oh, those things," he replied.

"What else did you have in mind?"

Quintin shrugged broad shoulders under his black sand-washed silk shirt. "Nothing. Nothing," he mumbled.

He had barely registered the furnishings in the other rooms. He was too busy trying to sort out his reaction to Victoria Jones. What was it about his neighbor that made him feel and react like a gauche adolescent?

He was certain he was more worldly than she, but there was a strange wisdom about Victoria that made him doubt she would ever lose her cool no matter what the circumstances.

She had ventured into a career in what most considered a man's domain and she had survived. Not only was she beautiful, but she was also bright and confident.

"That concludes the tour," Victoria stated, leading Quintin down the hall to the staircase.

Quintin spent the next hour sipping champagne and sampling the exquisite hors d'oeuvres Victoria had prepared. He bit into a grape leaf stuffed with goat cheese, pine nuts, and currants. He followed that with smoked salmon and caviar on toast points.

"This is definitely X-rated food," he sighed.

"It is a bit sensual," Victoria agreed.

He thought of it as downright erotic. His lids lowered as he studied Victoria in the way he usually studied a model. The food she had prepared as well as the white silk outfit she wore were all erotic. Even her hair—curled softly around her face—was erotic.

He stared at her over the rim of his fluted glass, a slight smile lifting the corners of his mouth. "I must admit that I'm enjoying your music."

Victoria laughed openly. "I didn't think you'd appreciate my taste in music."

"It isn't something I would buy, but it'll do."

"What do you like?"

"The blues and R&B."

"Not that stuff you were blasting yesterday?" she asked, wrinkling her nose.

"Exactly. B. B. King, Otis Redding, Bobby Blue Bland, Wilson Pickett, Aretha Franklin, James Brown . . ."

"I get the picture," Victoria said, grimacing.

"What's wrong with them?"

"Nothing, Quintin."

He saw her lips twitch in amusement as she turned her head. "Could it be, Miss Victoria Jones, that you're lying to me?"

Victoria managed a straight face. "Never, Mr. Lord."

Quintin stared at her, pleased to note the sadness had left her gaze. He wondered who or what had hurt her so deeply that it was mirrored in her eyes. Reaching over, he refilled her glass with the pale, sparkling wine. He had refilled his own glass three times to her one, and he was beginning to feel the effects of the champagne.

"Would you like to view the paintings?" he asked. He had to get up, do anything except sit and stare at Victoria Jones. She was delicate. Hypnotic. Her body was tiny and perfectly formed, her face young and innocent. Her voice was soft, feminine and controlled; perhaps too controlled.

Victoria's large eyes widened perceptibly. "Yes, Quintin."

He rose to his feet, seemingly in slow motion. It seemed like hours, but it took only minutes for him to retrieve the drawings from the case he had left by his front door. Hannibal blinked slowly at him, licked his whiskers, then promptly went back to sleep. Quintin had explained to Hannibal that he was going next door—alone.

Victoria cleared a portion of the dining-room table, and when Quintin returned, she watched him lay out the watercolor drawings.

She caught her lower lip between her teeth as her heart pounded wildly. Quintin Lord was right. He was very, very good! The images seemed to jump at her while pulling her in at the same time. The soft muted shades of a lavender and indigo sky cradled the stark branches of white birch trees in the blazing splendor of a setting sun, firing the land with reds, raw sienna, ocher browns, and green.

Quintin felt rather than saw her reaction to the painting. "If you like this one the next one should really please you," he stated confidently.

He was right. That one was also a landscape, with purple hills and stark white birch trees swayed by the force of a rushing orange and yellow waterfall. Droplets of water dotted the trees like sprinkling snow. The background was mauve, pinks, and soft lavenders. Instead of an orange sun there was an orange moon. The painting was large; perfect for her living room.

"I want it, Quintin." She was hard pressed to keep the excitement from her voice.

He rested his hand on her shoulder in a possessive gesture. "It's yours."

Turning slightly, Victoria stared up at him. "How much do I owe you?"

"Nothing," he whispered.

"Nothing?" she repeated.

"Nothing, Victoria."

"No," she protested, shaking her head. "I can't—"

"It's a housewarming gift," Quintin cut in.

"But you can sell it—"

"I'll never sell it," he interrupted again.

Her feelings for this man intensified with every moment she spent in his presence, but there was no way she wanted to be obligated to him—not for anything.

"Have you shown this to anybody?"

"No."

"Why not?"

Quintin shrugged a shoulder. "I never got around to it."

"That's why you haven't sold it," Victoria stated with a smugness she didn't actually feel.

His hand moved from her shoulder to her neck, then to her chin, lifting her face to his. "If you insist on buying it, then I'm more than willing to negotiate the terms, Miss Victoria Jones," he said, lowering his head.

Victoria felt the hardness of his chest against her breasts, the strength of his fingers around her waist, and the mastery of his mouth as it worked its magic on her lips.

She became a part of Quintin, feeling what she felt when she saw his paintings—being pulled in and floating in and out of hot and cool colors of orange and lavender.

The hair on his upper lip was startling, totally masculine and masterful. She groaned, inhaling, and her lips parted. His tongue moved tentatively into her mouth, then withdrew.

Raising his head slightly, he stared down into her startled gaze. "That was only the down payment. I'll take the rest in twelve equal installments," he teased with a smile.

Victoria's shoulders shook uncontrollably. She couldn't stop laughing as she rested her forehead against Quintin's chest. Slender arms encircling his waist, she collapsed against his body.

"You're impossible, Quintin."

He rested his chin on the top of her head. "No, Vicky, I'm good; very good."

Placing both hands against his chest, she gave him a gentle push. "I think I need some leverage in this deal."

Quintin's lids lowered slightly over his gold-brown eyes. "Are you proposing a counteroffer?"

"How would you like to put away some of your take-out menus for a while?"

His smile was wide and dazzling. "Are you saying you'll cook for me?"

She nodded. "I have to cook for myself, so I'll just prepare a little extra for you."

"You've got yourself a deal." He released her and reached for the painting. "I'll frame this and hang it for you."

"Thank you, Quintin."

He stared at Victoria, nodding. *Don't thank me,* he thought. He should be the one thanking her; thanking her because for the first time in a long time he wanted a woman, and wanted her for more than a sexual encounter.

The night had begun and ended well—for the both of them.

Five

Victoria opened her apartment door early Saturday morning to the announcement of a flower delivery at the same time a tall, beautiful, pencil-thin woman quietly closed the door to Quintin's apartment. The woman flashed a mysterious smile, slipped on a pair of over-size sunglasses, and strutted sensuously down the hallway and out of the building.

Victoria exhaled, smiling. It appeared as if Quintin Lord was involved with a woman, and knowing this would remind her not get too involved with her neighbor.

The delivery of flowers from a local florist was quickly followed by a second delivery from a nursery that left a towering sequoia cactus, with a note from her parents. She directed the nurserymen to position the tree near the sliding-glass doors leading to a spacious patio, which spanned the length of the kitchen, living, and dining rooms. This signaled the delivery of several more large house plants and exquisite serving pieces she could use when entertaining.

She prepared green salads, set up the serving tables on the patio, thankful that the weather was warm, with sunny skies and a hint of a cooling breeze. Selecting background music, a variety of differing wines, arranging flowers, and wiping away a light layer of dust from the cherry-wood furniture took up most of the morning. Glancing at the kitchen clock, she knew she only had an hour before her guests were due to arrive. Since most of her friends lived in the D.C. area, she had decided on a luncheon instead of a dinner.

Forty-five minutes later, Victoria, dressed in a silk T-shirt in a flattering apricot color and a sweeping black silk chiffon skirt of many layers, opened the door to her father and mother.

At sixty-eight and sixty-six respectively, William and Marion Jones's exuberance and stylish elegance belied their ages. William, a former ambassador to Seychelles and Togo, and Marion, a former French teacher, had taken their newly retired status seriously. Both of them had become avid golfers.

"Welcome, Mom and Dad," Victoria said, greeting her parents warmly. "Thank you for the cactus."

Marion Jones's dark brown eyes darted quickly around the entryway as she made her way into the living room. "I like it, sweetheart," she said, examining the cathedral ceiling and the light pouring in through floor-to-ceiling windows.

William Jones folded his daughter into a rib-crushing embrace, lifting her easily off her feet. "You've done it, honey."

Victoria kissed her father's smooth jaw. "And you didn't think I could."

William smiled, nodding his head. "I knew you could. It's just that I feel better knowing you're not living alone in some isolated part of the city."

"I do live alone," Victoria retorted, frowning up at William after he'd released her. Aware of her father's outdated belief that women shouldn't live alone or that they needed a man to protect them, she quickly changed the topic. "Come and see how I've decorated the upstairs," she suggested.

Petite silver-haired Marion smiled. "William and I will look around. You stay here and greet your guests."

Victoria knew her mother was annoyed. She only called her husband William when that was the case. Normally she would have called him Bill or sweetheart. Everyone was a "sweetheart" to Marion Jones.

William and Marion ascended the curving staircase and the doorbell chimed again. Victoria answered the ring, releasing the building's outer door, then waited for her best friend to make her way down the hall.

Red-haired Joanna Landesmann reminded Victoria of a sparkling penny. Her short hair was a shiny copper, her friendly eyes a bright clear brown, and a light sprinkling of freckles stood out across her pert nose and sculpted cheeks.

"Welcome!" Victoria called out, greeting Joanna with a warm smile and kiss on her cheek. "Thank you for the beautiful flowers and the punch bowl."

Joanna returned the kiss. "Glad you liked them. You just don't know how many times I drove past this place and wanted to stop by. But I managed to quell my inquisitiveness and waited for today."

"My, my, my. Have you changed, Miss Landesmann?"

Joanna affected a moue. "One must grow up one day."

At thirty, Joanna was mature except when it came to affairs of the heart. The professional party planner always seemed to pick the wrong man to fall in love with. Her boyfriends took advantage of her generous nature, breaking her heart before Joanna realized it was she who did all of the giving in their relationship.

Victoria led Joanna into the kitchen. "Who are you in love with now?"

"No one, and I don't expect there will be anyone for a long time. I've sworn off men."

"For how long?" Victoria couldn't help smiling.

"It's been over two months." Joanna's expression was more serious than sad.

This disclosure surprised Victoria. She and Joanna had

worked for the same hotel in Washington, D.C., and become fast friends from the first time Joanna, as banquet manager, conferred with Victoria, who as the sous chef monitored every station in the kitchen. The two women discovered they shared similar tastes in music, old movies, antique and craft shops. Like Victoria, Joanna eventually left the hotel to go into business for herself. Joanna still lived in D.C., but she and Victoria managed to get together every other month for lunch or dinner.

"What happened to that lobbyist, Jo?"

"I sent him packing. He was such a liar, and you know how I hate liars."

Victoria smiled. "Good for you."

Joanna returned her smile. "It felt good to give him his walking papers," she stated, glancing around the kitchen. "I don't believe this place. It's incredible."

Victoria nodded her thanks, experiencing twin feelings of pride and apprehension: pride because she was the only one controlling her career but some apprehension because she desperately wanted her catering enterprise to be a success.

The front doorbell chimed again, and Victoria went to answer it. Over the next half hour it chimed many more times. By two o'clock everyone had arrived and settled down to sample the different dishes Victoria Jones had prepared for the guests who had come to wish her well in her new home and new business endeavor.

Nathaniel Jones, co-anchor on a D.C. cable news station, dropped an arm around his sister's shoulder. Leaning over, he kissed Victoria's cheek. "Do you think you can whip up something special for Christine's parents' fortieth wedding anniversary?"

Victoria glanced over at her sister-in-law who was engaged in an animated conversation with the elder Joneses.

"You have to let me know how many people I'm serving and whether you want a sit-down dinner or a buffet."

"I think a buffet dinner is preferable."

"How many, Nat?"

"Christine has compiled a list of sixty-two."

Victoria curved an arm around her brother's waist. "I'll fix something nice."

"Low-fat sauces, no-cholesterol desserts, and low-sodium cheese spreads for the middle-age matrons please," he teased.

"I'm going to tell Christine what you've said."

"No, Vicky, don't. She claims at least once a day that I don't like her family."

Victoria smiled up at her tall, well-groomed, handsome brother. "But you don't, Nat Jones."

"That's because they are puffed-up snobs."

"Look who's talking," she retorted, snorting delicately and walking away. Nathaniel Jones was so conservative that he had earned the name Clark Kent. It followed him throughout his years as a Washington, D.C., journalist and now as a popular television news anchor.

Victoria mingled among her guests, graciously accepting their compliments on her cooking. Many of them had taken the elegant business cards she had left on the side tables in the living room.

Her sister Kimberly was the first to leave. She had to return to Silver Spring to breast-feed her three-month-old son. Victoria handed her a decorative bag filled with several containers of food.

"This is for Russell. He called earlier and asked for samples."

Kimberly laughed. The last thing her high school football coach husband needed was food. It was a constant battle for Russell Abernathy to keep his weight under two fifty.

"Maybe I'll tell him you forgot to give them to me," Kimberly said.

"I won't lie for you, Kimm."

"I thought sisters were supposed to stick together."

"Not when my brother-in-law can power lift me with one hand," Victoria countered with a wide grin.

Kimberly shrugged slender shoulders. "I guess it's the least I can do for him for babysitting."

"Kiss the baby for me, Kimm."

Kimberly noted the longing expression in her older sister's eyes. "I will. But why don't you come down and see him and kiss him yourself?"

Victoria averted her gaze. "I will. As soon as I settle in I'll be down."

It was a lie and both women knew it. Victoria had only seen her nephew once since his birth. She found it difficult to hold the tiny baby and not think of her own barren womb. She had come to the sad conclusion that she would never be able to claim as her own any baby she held.

Victoria hugged and kissed her sister. "Thank you for coming."

Kimberly held her close. "Thank you for inviting me."

The small crowd dispersed in groups of twos and threes over the next three hours, leaving Joanna and Victoria savoring cups of freshly brewed cappuccino.

Joanna anchored her feet on a rung of the tall stool in the kitchen. She licked a dot of frothy milk off her upper lip. "How would you like a partner?"

Victoria put down her cup, staring at her friend. "What are you talking about?"

Joanna blushed to the roots of her dark red hair. "Well, not exactly partners. But . . . something like a collaboration."

Resting her arms on the butcher-block countertop, Victoria's eyes narrowed. "What are you hatching, Jo?"

"I've done rather well putting together weddings, bridal showers, school reunions, and sweet sixteen parties. And I'm certain you're going to be a big success once word gets out that you cater these same events. And . . ."

"And?" Victoria asked when Joanna hesitated.

"I want to help you for helping me when I broke up with Addison Fletcher. What I'm trying to say is whenever I contract to do an event I'll recommend you as the caterer."

"That's not necessary, Jo. My business will come around in its own time."

"But why struggle to build it up when you can come out of the chute at full speed. I've managed to contract for at least two to three events a month and most of my contacts have been through referrals. I've even stopped spending money on advertising. I have a client who gives a luncheon for her bored and idle rich friends at least once a week. The woman spends nearly two hundred dollars a pop on flowers alone, while the firm that caters her food is horrific. They serve the same bland, boring food week after week."

Victoria picked up her cup, taking a sip of the fragrant coffee. "Apparently the bored and idle rich ladies are satisfied with the food being served."

"They can't be. They only come because Mrs. Sunny Calhoun is the social grande dame of Baltimore's National Preservation Society. Please, Victoria, let me talk to her about your services. She only has to try you once. If she doesn't like what you prepare she can always go back to the other caterers."

"Let me think . . ." The doorbell chimed melodiously, preempting what Victoria was going to say. "Excuse me, Jo."

She went to the door and opened it. Quintin Lord filled the doorway, an irresistibly devastating grin curving his mouth.

"Hi," Victoria whispered, her heart pounding loudly in her ears.

His gaze swept quickly over her face and body, missing nothing. "Hi," he returned, the single word soft and caressing. "I framed your picture. If you don't mind I'd like to hang it for you."

She stared up at him as if she had never seen him before. "If it's a bad time I'll come back later," Quintin said quickly.

Victoria inhaled sharply. Seeing Quintin Lord again was overwhelming to her senses. Whenever she was in his presence she couldn't ignore the tingle of excitement inside her. And at that moment it hadn't mattered that she saw a woman leaving his apartment earlier that day. This man—her neighbor—evoked passions she thought had faded when her marriage ended.

The realization washed over her. She wanted Quintin Lord!

"I . . . I have company," she stuttered.

Quintin pulled his gaze away from Victoria, focusing instead on the profusion of flowers, houseplants, and the seguro cactus near the patio doors. He had deliberately kept himself busy all day rather than think about her, but he had failed miserably.

When he least expected it, the image of Victoria Jones had crept unbiddingly into his mind, disrupting his concentration and causing his thoughts to wander. He had been so distracted that even his art students asked if he was feeling well. He'd said he was, but he wasn't.

He had spent the last twenty-four hours recalling the softness of her skin, the fragrance of her perfume, and the taste and feel of her mouth when he had kissed her.

Vicky Jones had gotten to him. The woman didn't appear to be the slightest bit interested in him, yet she had gotten to him.

I'm losing it, he thought, running a hand over his face, and at that moment he knew he had to do something without letting Victoria know what he had planned.

He lowered his hand, staring intently at her upturned face. "I'll come back later." He was so enthralled with her tiny body covered in silk and airy chiffon that he almost missed the tall red-haired woman making her way toward them.

Victoria noted the direction of Quintin's gaze and glanced over her shoulder. She turned back to him. "I'd like for you to meet a good friend of mine, Joanna Landesmann. Jo, this is Quintin Lord, my neighbor."

His attention temporarily diverted, Quintin extended his hand. "My pleasure."

Joanna grasped his hand, her clear brown eyes sweeping appreciatively over his face. "The pleasure is *mine,* Quintin."

Victoria registered a familiar tone in Joanna's voice. She was flirting with Quintin whether she was aware of it or not.

Quintin released Joanna's hand, his gold-brown gaze softening as he smiled down at Victoria. "I'll see you later." He nodded to Joanna. "Nice meeting you."

Victoria closed the door behind him, then turned to smile at a grinning Joanna.

"He's gorgeous," Joanna whispered.

"That he is," Victoria agreed solemnly.

"What are you going to do about it?"

"What in the world are you talking about?"

"Is he married?"

"I don't think so."

"Is he engaged?" Joanna continued.

"I don't know."

"Find out, Miss Jones!"

"Why should I?"

"Because you need a man."

Laughing, Victoria shook her head. "Now you're beginning to sound like my father. I don't need a man."

"How long has it been, my friend? Two, maybe three years?"

"And it'll be even longer, Jo. Right now I don't have time for a relationship."

Joanna folded her arms over her chest, giving Victoria a questioning look. "What's wrong, Vicky? You dated that representative from Ohio, but you broke it off just when the man was ready to propose to you. Then there was that undersecretary from the Defense Department who was here one day and gone the next."

Victoria wanted to scream at Joanna to mind her own business. There was no way she could explain to her friend that she didn't want to become involved with a man because the moment they mentioned marriage and children she rejected them. They'd want children and she couldn't have children, and there weren't too many men who were willing to adopt someone else's child.

Joanna glanced down at her watch. "I think I'd better be getting back before I run into D.C. traffic. Thanks again for the invite."

Victoria flashed a warm smile, then hugged Joanna. "Thank you for coming. And I promise I'll think about your offer to go in with you."

Joanna's face brightened with a smile. "Please do. I think we'd make a dynamic duo."

"Like Batman and Robin," Victoria quipped.

"Tarzan and Jane," Joanna countered.

"Abbott and Costello."

"Peaches and Herb," Joanna shot back.

"Desi and Lucy," Victoria said, giggling.

"Ike and Tina," Joanna sputtered.

"Not!" they both chorused, laughing.

Joanna picked up her large handbag. "I'm out of here."

Victoria walked her to the door and waited until she walked down the hall and out into the warm Baltimore evening.

The door to Quintin's apartment stood open, and Hannibal ambled out and sniffed at Victoria's legs. Leaning over, she scratched him behind his ears.

"Hey, Hannibal. How are you?"

Hannibal responded with a loud bark and moved closer to her.

"Don't jump, Hannibal" came a stern command behind her.

She turned around and smiled up at Quintin. "He didn't jump on me this time."

Quintin's gaze was fixed on her mouth. "I gave him a lecture about jumping on you."

"It's obvious that he's quite obedient."

Quintin shifted a black eyebrow. "He's been trained to obey."

Her heart started up its uneven rhythm again. There was a tangible bond between her and this man that was so apparent and startling, it robbed her of speech and reason.

His gaze moved with agonizing slowness from her mouth to her throat, then down to her chest. Victoria felt her breasts tingle against the silky fabric of her T-shirt.

The man was making love to her without touching her. How was that possible?

She stared back with longing and there was no way she could hide her desire for him from him.

"Have you eaten?" she asked, her voice a throaty whisper. Quintin shook his head, not daring to speak, move, or break the spell he'd woven without his being aware of it.

Victoria swallowed painfully. "I'll fix you a plate."

Quintin had to move. She walked past him and into her apartment, leaving him staring after her, his fists clenched tightly.

Turning, he walked stiffly into his apartment, his rebellious body betraying him. He'd lied. He wanted Victoria Jones for herself and for sex. He *was* lusting after the woman.

Six

Victoria stood at the doorway to Quintin's apartment, holding a tray filled with several covered dishes. Hannibal rose from his lounging position at the door, his soft whining alerting Quintin someone had invaded the canine's territory.

"Come in, Vicky."

She stepped into the entryway, noting most of the previous clutter was missing; however, half-completed canvases were still lined up against the living-room walls while a camera perched on a tripod was positioned in the middle of the room.

Quintin appeared and took the tray from her hands and placed it on a table. "Are you going to join me?"

"No," she said quickly. "I've eaten."

"How was your housewarming?"

"A smashing success."

Quintin shifted his eyebrows. "A smashing success," he repeated, smiling. "You sound like a Brit."

Victoria gave him a saucy grin. "Would you prefer that I'd said it was all that?"

Throwing back his head, he laughed. "I never would've thought you'd know any street slang."

"Why?" She managed to look insulted.

"Because of your taste in music, Miss Jones."

"What's wrong with my taste in music?"

"It's all wrong. It has no feeling, no passion and no soul."

"And yours does?"

"Yup," he said smugly. "You can feel my music. It pulls you in and sweeps you along with the rhythm, not releasing you until the last note fades away."

"That's your opinion, Mr. Lord."

He sobered. "And it's my opinion that you're a fabulous cook and a very beautiful woman."

Victoria was caught off guard by his compliment, but somewhere she managed to find herself and her voice. "Thank you, Quintin."

He nodded, smiling. "At least we can agree on that," he said softly, staring back at her in a waiting silence. "I'd like to contract your services for a dinner party."

"When, where, and for how many?"

Quintin slipped his hands into the back pockets of his jeans. "Wednesday evening. Here, and dinner for two."

Victoria's breath caught in her lungs. He had just complimented her, then within the same breath asked that she cook for him and another woman. She recovered quickly.

"What do you want me to prepare?"

"I'll leave that up to you?"

"You must have a preference—fish, poultry, or red meat."

"A shellfish appetizer and a poultry entrée. Any vegetable and dessert you choose will do."

"Do you want me to provide wine or liqueurs?"

"Yes to both. In fact, Victoria, I want you to select everything from the food, to the music and anything else I'd need to make a favorable and lasting impression on a woman."

She forced back a grimace. The Cheshire cat grin on the face of the woman leaving his apartment earlier that morning spoke volumes. Her expression indicated not only had Quintin impressed her, but he had also satisfied her.

She flashed a false smile, admitting to herself that she couldn't afford to be distracted by romantic notions.

"You intend to entertain a woman in this . . . this . . . this . . . *hovel?*"

Quintin shrugged wide shoulders. "I paint, Miss Jones, not keep house."

"Then you should hire a housekeeper," Victoria shot back, not caring whether he heard the censure in her voice.

"Hire one for me," he countered, struggling not to laugh.

"I'll do just that." Victoria spun around on her heel and walked out of his apartment and back into her own, the sound of his laughter following her and echoing in her head.

When she slammed her door, she thought how the sound resembled the crack of a rifle.

Fool!

She had been a fool to give Quintin Lord even a passing thought even though he had kissed her. Besides, they had nothing in common; they were complete opposites.

Maybe Jo was right. She had been without male company for too long and she was desperate.

But she wasn't desperate; she was alone by choice not because she couldn't attract a man.

Her eyes widened and she bit down on her lower lip to keep from laughing hysterically when she thought about attracting a man.

She would make certain Quintin Lord wouldn't pay any attention to his long-legged date or his meal.

Wednesday night would be a night to remember—for everyone.

Victoria inspected Quintin's kitchen and living and dining rooms, declaring it all clean and tidy and paid the cleaning woman she had called for her services.

"It looks rather nice, doesn't it?" Quintin remarked as he stared down at the shining surface of his dining-room table. "I don't think I've seen the top of this table for months."

That's because you live like a slob, Victoria thought. She managed to give him a saccharine grin.

"I'm going to take Hannibal over to my sister for the night," Quintin stated evenly, examining her enchanting profile.

"Why? Doesn't he like your girlfriend?" she questioned. Hannibal stared up at her, whining softly.

"They like each other a little too well and I don't want to compete with my pet for a woman's attention."

Turning, she glanced up at Quintin. Hannibal might like Quintin's girlfriend, but Victoria doubted she would make a similar impression with the woman. "What time do you want me to serve dinner?"

"Eight. If you need to set up anything before then, just walk in. I'll leave the door open."

"I'll probably begin setting up about seven forty-five." She wiggled her fingers at him and gave him a wink. "I'll see you later."

Victoria wasn't as concerned about the dishes she had selected for Quintin's dinner party as she was about her own appearance. She had prepared everything she was to serve Quintin and his dining partner, but she didn't have much time to fix her face and hair.

She showered and washed her hair in record time. But she used the better part of an hour to blow out her hair and curl it with a curling iron. The tiny curls bounced around head and forehead as she picked them out with her fingertips.

Victoria moisturized her body with a creamy, scented lotion and added a dot of perfume behind her ears, at the base of her throat, on her inner wrists, and behind her knees.

A mischievous smile softened her lush mouth when she eased her slender body into a white tank dress. The body-hugging garment revealed every curve of her petite frame. She had changed underpants several times before she found a pair that would not show under the snug dress. The dark brown lace bikini panties were as equally risqué as the dress that ended six inches above her knees.

Making up her face, utilizing the professional techniques she'd learned years before when she had performed on stage, Victoria highlighted her best features.

Satisfied with the results, she slipped her bare feet into a pair of black patent-leather sling-back sandals. The three-inch heels made her dress appear even shorter. All the better, she thought.

Running her fingers through her hair again and fluffing the curls, she smiled at her reflection in the bathroom mirror. She washed her hands, dried them, then descended the stairs to serve Quintin Lord and his date.

At exactly seven forty-five Victoria pushed a serving cart into the neighboring apartment. Quintin was nowhere to be seen. She spread a lace tablecloth over the dining-room table, and set the table with china, silver, crystal, and cloth napkins. Next, she arranged a bouquet of delicate yellow roses in a crystal vase that doubled as a centerpiece. Lemon-scented candles, dimmed overhead chandelier, a bottle of white wine chilling in a silver bucket, and a compact disc playing soft music set the mood when Quintin finally made his way down the staircase.

He saw the vision in white bending over the table, re-arranging glasses and silverware, and he nearly lost his footing. Victoria was clothed, yet every curve of her body was outlined by the form-fitting tank dress. She couldn't have turned him on more if she had been naked.

He stared numbly, appraising her perfect legs in the high heels. The muted light caught the smooth darkness of her exposed flesh, making it a shimmering brown satin.

His gaze moved slowly over her flat belly, her rounded hips, and the soft fullness of her small breasts.

Victoria glanced up. When she saw him, her smile flashed sensuous and mysterious. "How does it look?"

"Beautiful. Beautiful," he repeated, coming closer.

Somewhere in the living room a clock chimed softly. It was eight o'clock.

Victoria stared up at Quintin, stunned by his appearance. Again, he was dressed in black, but this time his attire was linen instead of silk.

His jaw was clean-shaven, his hair soft and shiny, and the smell emanating from him was clean, manly, and intoxicating.

"Your date is late," she stated quietly.

Quintin's hands came up slowly and his fingers curved around her bare upper arms. "No, she isn't." He stared deeply into her eyes. "You're my date, Vicky."

Victoria would've fallen if Quintin hadn't tightened his hold on her arms. He pulled her closer until her breasts were flattened against the hardness of his chest.

Lowering her head, she began to laugh. So much for making his date jealous. Her plan had backfired.

"You tricked me, Quintin."

Pressing his mouth to her forehead, he kissed her curls. "I'm sorry about that. I'll try and make it up to you," he crooned.

Tilting her chin, she stared longingly into the depths of his sherry-colored eyes. "How?"

"I'll begin with this." His head came down and his mouth covered hers gently yet masterfully.

Her slender arms wound around his waist, her feminine heat and fragrance sweeping over him.

The feel of his thick, silken mustache sent shock waves

throughout her nervous system as his tongue searched out hers, capturing it in a dance of desire.

Quintin cradled Victoria's face between his hands, afraid to touch her body, for if he touched her he would never have the opportunity to romance her. She would end up sharing his bed. It wasn't that he didn't want to sleep with her, but it was too soon. She was different from the other women he had gone out with, and that was something he could not forget.

Victoria felt the heat, a ripple of excitement, and the rising passion. Her whole being seemed to be poised, waiting for something she hadn't experienced in a long time.

She was waiting for fulfillment; a fulfillment that was just out of reach.

A fulfillment she wanted to experience, but not yet. It was too soon.

"Quint, please," she murmured against his searching, questing lips.

Quintin's fingers threaded sensuously through her hair, his fingertips massaging her scalp and causing her nerves to come alive in a warm, tingling sensation.

Unconsciously, she pressed closer while praying he would release her. If he didn't let her go she would embarrass herself. She didn't want to beg him to make love to her.

He released her mouth but not her head, and Victoria buried her face against his hard chest, trying to bring her emotions under control.

"I think I've just paid for the watercolor—in full," she breathed out in a heavy sigh.

"I don't think so, Vicky."

"Why?" she crooned, inhaling his after-shave.

"You tried to seduce me."

Pulling back, Victoria stared up at him. "I did not try to seduce you."

"Then what do you call this . . . this postage stamp-size garment pasted on your body?"

She managed to look insulted. "It's a dress, Quintin."

"Yeah, right. And I'm Michelangelo di Lodovico Buonarroti Simoni."

"And I love your ceiling," she countered softly.

"Don't try to change the topic, Miss Jones. Were you or were you not trying to seduce me?"

"No," she answered truthfully. She wasn't trying to seduce Quintin. She just wanted to make his date jealous. "Come, it's time to eat."

What Quintin wanted to eat was not on tonight's menu, but this wouldn't be the last time Victoria Jones would find herself in his arms. After all they were neighbors and there was no way they could avoid each other.

Seven

Victoria felt Quintin watching her every motion. She was thoroughly embarrassed. She had worn the skimpy dress to divert some of the attention away from his so-called date but unknowingly she had garnered his attention—all of it.

Bending down, she unloaded a lower shelf of the serving cart and placed a bowl of a three-pepper salad on the table, along with an accompanying lobster, papaya, and avocado salad on crisp red-leaf lettuce leaves.

Straightening, she folded her hands on her hips, the toe of one shoe tapping angrily on the floor. "Have you seen enough?"

Biting down on his lower lip to stifle his laughter, Quintin nodded slowly. "For now." He extended a hand. "Come sit down. I won't have you waiting on me."

"But you're paying me to wait on you," she retorted.

"There's going to be a slight modification. Tonight I'm paying for your cooking and your company."

Taking his hand, Victoria allowed him to seat her. He took a chair to her right at the head of the table, flashing a grin.

"I knew what you were up to the moment I saw you in that dress," Quintin confessed.

"You . . . you couldn't," Victoria sputtered, heat flaming her cheeks.

Lowering his chin, he gave her a long, knowing look.

"You didn't dress like that the other night when you invited me to your place, so I figured you wanted to make a statement."

Bracing her elbows on the table, she rested her chin on her fists. "What did I want to say?"

His gaze swept leisurely over her face. "That you're *all* woman, Vicky Jones."

Oh, how wrong you are, she thought. *I may look like a woman but there is something missing.*

Schooling her features not to reveal her inner turmoil, she managed a false grin. "Guilty as charged."

Quintin reached for the bottle of wine and removed the cork effortlessly. He poured the fragrant pale liquid in her glass, then filled his own. Lowering his head slightly, he gave her a sidelong glance. Victoria found the gesture not only charming but endearing.

"Do you dress like *this* for other men?" His voice was quiet, and heavy with sarcasm.

Victoria unfolded her napkin and placed it on her lap. "On occasion," she replied truthfully.

"On how many occasions?"

Her lashes swept up and she gave him an innocent look. "A couple," she answered with a shrug of a bare shoulder.

Quintin's mouth tightened under his mustache. Victoria Jones was a flirt *and* a tease.

"May I make a request, Victoria?"

She raised her delicate eyebrows, giving him an expression of innocence that disarmed him immediately. "Of course, Quintin."

"I . . ." He hesitated, not wanting her to think he was domineering or a chauvinist. He chose his words carefully. "Will you not wear that dress or anything quite that fitted if you . . . you agree to go out with me."

Victoria glanced down at her dress. "You think this is too tight?" she asked with an incredulous look on her face, unable to resist teasing him.

"You bet your . . ."

Her head came up slowly. "My what?" she drawled with an exaggerated flutter of her lashes.

Quintin's thunderous expression vanished when he realized she was teasing him. Leaning closer, he trailed his left hand over her silken cheek. "You can bet your tutu it's too tight."

Both of them laughed at the alliteration and their laughter set the mood for the evening.

Quintin was effusive in his praise as he tasted each dish she had prepared. He had never developed a taste for avocado, but its pairing with the flaky succulent lobster meat and the sweet papaya juice in a tarragon vinegar and delicate olive oil sauce changed his mind.

He took a forkful of hoppin' John, biting into a succulent shrimp. "Oh, Vicky," he moaned, closing his eyes. "This is better than my mother's."

"I decided to add a Cajun touch with the shrimp and spices," she informed him.

Quintin took another forkful. "Yup. I think you've outdone Mrs. Etta Mae Lord."

Victoria laughed at Quintin's boyish banter. He looked like a child in a bakery. "I take it your mother is a good cook?"

"One of the best," he admitted. "She had enough practice cooking for a husband and nine children."

She blinked slowly, her mouth gaping. "You're one of nine?"

"Six boys and three girls," he said proudly.

"You could've been a baseball team."

"The Lords were quite a handful. However, no one, and I mean *no one,* crossed Etta Mae Lord. She made certain we were clean, cooked wonderful meals, and kept everyone in line with just a look. It was my father who was the teddy bear. His favorite saying was, 'Etta Mae, let up on them. After all, they're only children.' He had no way of knowing that if his wife had let up on the children he probably would've had to ask permission to enter his own house."

Victoria's eyes were crinkled with laughter. "Where are you in the birth order?"

"Fifth. My folks had six boys before they got their first girl. Then they decided to try again and it was another girl and then another."

"Why did they stop at nine?"

"They ran out of bedrooms. Our house had six bedrooms, including a nursery, and my mother felt two kids to each bedroom was enough. She believed the eldest boy and girl should have their own rooms, so that left the others to double up."

"It sounds as if you had a lot of fun."

Quintin smiled, nodding. He cheerfully related the scrapes and episodes they managed to hide from their eagle-eyed, perceptive mother, who at times threatened she was going to find a job outside of the house and leave her offspring to fend for themselves.

"Her threat was taken quite seriously," he continued. "My mother had a nursing degree, and she could've always worked per diem at a local hospital, but she gave up her career to become a homemaker. So whenever she talked about getting a *real job,* we always solicited our dad's support, and he firmly made his point when he told Etta Mae he worked a sixteen-hour day just to make certain his wife could stay at home and take care of his children."

"What does your father do?"

"He owns an auto repair shop." Quintin registered Victoria's serene expression and slight smile. She was delicate and alluring, and it was the first time she appeared totally relaxed and at ease with him.

"Tell me about the Joneses." He took a sip of wine,

silently admiring the flickering glow of the soft candlelight on her satiny skin.

"There's not much to tell," Victoria began. "I'm one of three, and the middle child. I have an older brother who is a journalist and a younger sister who's a teacher.

"My parents are both retired and they're thinking about a second career as amateur golfers."

"What were their first careers?"

"My mother was a French teacher and my father worked for the State Department. He was an ambassador to Seychelles and Togo."

This disclosure intrigued Quintin. "Did you live in Africa?"

"No," she replied, shaking her head. "My father was too uneasy about the political structure of these newly independent countries to have his family live with him on a permanent basis. We visited on our school holidays and during the summer."

"It must have been fascinating." Quintin's expressive gold-brown eyes were shining. "I've always wanted to be part of a sailing expedition to Africa."

"Sail?" Victoria gave him a skeptical look. "Why not fly?"

"Because I'd rather sail." Leaning back slightly, he crossed his arms over his chest. "I have to admit that I like sailing more than anything else in the world. It's become somewhat of an addiction."

"How long have you had this addiction?"

Resting his arms on the table, he leaned closer to Victoria. "All of my life, Dr. Jones," he whispered quietly.

"Have you done anything to assuage this somewhat unusual craving, Mr. Lord?" she returned in a soft, soothing tone, playing along with him.

"Yup," he replied, nodding slowly.

She leaned closer. "How?"

"I bought a boat."

It was Victoria's turn to arch her eyebrows. "A sailboat?"

"A cruiser."

"Where do you keep it?"

"I have a slip down at a marina near the harbor. Have you ever been to the Keys?" She shook her head in the negative. "How would you like to sail down one weekend?" he asked.

Victoria stared at the expectant expression on Quintin's face. She wanted so much to refuse his offer but couldn't. His easygoing, relaxed manner was stirring and magnetic. With Quintin she never had to be on guard. She could be who she was without measuring every word or every gesture. She could be Victoria Jones and no one else.

"I'd like that very much."

Quintin let out his breath slowly, nodding, and his bright smile mirrored his intense pleasure. Everything he'd planned was falling into place. His newest craving was about to be assuaged. He would have Victoria Jones where he wanted her—on his boat, out on the ocean, miles from land.

"Do you have anything planned for next weekend?" he queried.

She mentally visualized her calendar, remembering she had to plan for her brother's in-laws' wedding anniversary fête.

"No. I'm free," she confirmed.

"Good. We'll leave early Friday morning and come back Sunday night."

Victoria ignored the warning that drew her to Quintin Lord, telling herself that he was her neighbor and they were complete opposites. There was no way she could become involved with him. Like the other men who'd been in her life since she'd ended her marriage, she would keep him at a distance.

It was with much reluctance Quintin dropped his gaze from Victoria's face, asking, "What's for dessert?"

Victoria rinsed the dusting of flour off her hands and picked up the telephone after the fourth ring.

"Miss Jones?" came an unfamiliar female voice on the other line.

"Speaking," she answered, cradling the receiver between her chin and shoulder.

"Miss Jones," the woman continued, "your name and number were given to Dr. Pearson by Mr. Quintin Lord, who's here recovering from emergency oral surgery."

Victoria's stomach made a flip-flop motion. "Is . . . is he all right?"

"He's fine, Miss Jones. It's just that he won't be able to drive home because of the anesthesia. Dr. Pearson would like to know if you'd be responsible for seeing that Mr. Lord gets home."

She glanced up at the kitchen clock. It was nearly four o'clock. "Of course." She wrote down the address of the oral surgeon, then hung up. Seconds later she dialed the number to a local taxi service, giving them her address and telling them to pick her up in ten minutes.

After changing into a pair of jeans and a yellow T-shirt, Victoria brushed her hair and covered it with a matching yellow painter's cap.

She hadn't seen or heard from Quintin in two days. He'd escorted her back to her apartment the night of their dinner party, giving her a chaste kiss on the cheek and a generous check to cover the cost of her preparing dinner and the cleaning woman's services.

The following morning there was no thumping music coming from the neighboring apartment or the sound of Hannibal's barking. The next day was a repeat of the day before. Victoria rang Quintin's doorbell, but received no response. Shrugging a shoulder, she returned to her own apartment, temporarily dismissing her elusive neighbor.

The taxi sped through downtown Baltimore, weaving dangerously in and out of rush-hour traffic. She paid the driver and walked into a modern office building.

Making her way through the mass of humanity flowing out of the air-conditioned building and into the city's humidity, Victoria found an elevator that took her to the eighth floor and the professional offices of Dr. Arnold Pearson.

Dr. Pearson handed her a printed sheet of paper. "Please follow the instructions on this page, Miss Jones. It is imperative that Mr. Lord not rinse his mouth for twenty-four hours. He shouldn't smoke, drink hot liquids, or attempt to drink through a straw. I don't want him to interfere with the normal clotting process; however, if there's excessive bleeding be certain to call my emergency number. Please remind him that he's to come back in a week for a follow-up visit. I'm also going to give you a prescription for a pain reliever. He's to take one tablet every four hours as needed."

Victoria stared numbly as the dentist handed her a prescription. She had to fill the prescription, drive Quintin home, then see that he followed all of the oral surgeon's instructions.

Slipping the prescription in her pocket, she smiled up at the dentist. "May I see Mr. Lord?" She followed him to a small room. Quintin lay on a bed, eyes closed and the left side of his face swollen from the packing cushioning his gum and jaw. Moving to his side, she touched his hand. His drug-glazed eyes opened immediately as he managed a grimace.

Victoria's delicate fingers went to his forehead, and she noted the growth of whiskers on his unshaven cheeks. Smiling, she leaned over his prone figure, her warm, haunting fragrance washing over him and helping Quintin to temporarily forget his discomfort.

She had come. He didn't know why, but somehow in the drug-induced nightmare he'd just experienced he thought she wouldn't come.

"I'm taking you home," she said quietly.

Quintin nodded and allowed Victoria to help him from the bed. Leaning heavily against her, he dropped an arm over her shoulders and placed one foot in front of the other. An emotion he'd never felt before struck a vibrant chord in him. He had deliberately stayed away from Victoria for the past two days, sailing aimlessly along Chesapeake Bay until an unexplained pain in the back of his mouth forced him back to land. Leaving Hannibal with his sister, he drove to the dentist. After a brief examination he had undergone emergency oral surgery for an impacted wisdom tooth.

He'd run from Victoria, but it had been useless. He needed her and he wanted her; but more than that he realized he was falling in love with her.

Eight

Quintin spent the next sixteen hours groping through a fog of darkness, warmth, and a softly crooning female voice. The only thing he was certain of was that he wasn't in his own bed. The scent and softness that was Victoria Jones surrounded him each time he surfaced from his drugged sleep.

Opening his eyes, he turned his head slowly. A hint of a smile crinkled his eyes but not his frightfully swollen jaw. It took herculean effort but he pushed himself into a sitting position. The motion caught Victoria's attention and she raised her head from the book she had been reading.

"Good morning." Her voice was soft and inviting.

Quintin mumbled a good morning, falling back weakly to the mound of pillows behind his head.

Victoria rose from a pale-green-and-white striped love seat and made her way across the bedroom to the bed. Bright sunlight pouring through the floor-to-ceiling windows shadowed her figure in brilliance as she moved closer to where Quintin had spent the night sleeping comfortably with the aid of the white pill she had given him.

Sitting down on the bed, she placed a cool hand on his forehead. Her dark eyes moved quickly over his face. The gauze packing had been removed from his mouth, yet the left side of his face remained grotesquely swollen, and some discoloration was evident along his jawline.

"Are you hungry?" Her warm breath washed over his face.

Quintin nodded. It had been more than twenty-four hours since he had eaten. The toothache had begun the morning after his dinner date with Victoria but he had ignored it. The throbbing pain continued off and on, prohibiting him from eating any solid foods. The discomfort grew progressively worse until he was blinded by the pain, and what he couldn't understand was that his last dental examination four months ago hadn't picked up anything.

"I'll make something soft for you to eat." Her gaze was filled with gentle concern. "Do you want something for the pain?" Victoria questioned.

"No more," he moaned, shaking his head. He didn't like the feeling of helplessness and not being in control. The tooth was gone, and it wouldn't be long before the pain also disappeared.

Victoria walked out of the bedroom, making her way down the winding staircase. After leaving the dentist, she had managed to get Quintin into his four-wheeler and struggled to support his sagging body enough to secure him with the seat belt. He'd slept while she stopped at a pharmacy to fill the prescription, waking only when she parked the auto at the rear of their house. He remained conscious long enough for her to open the door to her apartment where she pulled and pushed him up the staircase. She had decided to let him sleep in her guest bedroom so that she could monitor his recovery, but they never made it. Quintin collapsed at the top of the stairs, nearly crushing her when she fell under his solid body. It took another ten minutes to anchor her hands under his shoulders to pull him across the floor and into the bedroom that was closest to the staircase—her bedroom.

Quintin lay on the carpeted floor for an hour before waking again. He'd mumbled incoherently as she coaxed him onto the bed and removed his clothing. He swallowed one of the pills and promptly fell into a deep, painless slumber.

She had spent the night on the convertible love seat, sleeping fitfully and listening for a sound from the bed. Quintin had slept without waking throughout the night while she awoke feeling fatigued and aching. Her well-conditioned body had suffered the effects of her trying to move a man who weighed at least one hundred and seventy-five pounds.

Victoria returned to the bedroom with a bowl of lukewarm creamy oatmeal filled with applesauce and milk. She set the tray down on the bedside table, then handed Quintin a warm cloth and towel to clean and dry his face. When she sensed he seemed embarrassed by the gesture, hesitating to take the cloth, she turned her back to straighten the bed covering.

"Feeling better?" she asked, folding back the white eyelet comforter.

"Yes-s," he slurred, managing to wash his face, though unable to open his mouth comfortably.

She turned back to him, taking the cloth and towel. Smiling, she placed the tray across his lap. "You have another six hours before you'll be able to rinse your mouth with warm saltwater."

Quintin picked up a spoon. "I need to shave and take a shower," he mumbled.

Victoria smiled at him. "After you eat I'll help you."

His eyes widened and he shook his head. "No." He wouldn't mind Victoria helping him shower or even sharing a shower with her, but only if he was in control of his every thought and action.

She saw the frown settle into his features as he stared back at her. Her gaze inched down from his face to his bare chest. The sheet had fallen to his waist, and for the first time Victoria Jones felt the impact of the sensuality of the half-naked man in her bed. His shoulders were broad, his chest hard and furred with coarse black hair which tapered down to a narrow line over a flat belly, and his arms were long and ropy with lean, hard muscles.

She had realized all along, of course, Quintin Lord was a man but it was only now that she saw him as all *male.* She herself was female; a female who had denied her femininity for years. When had it all happened and why had she allowed herself to wallow and drown in self-doubt?

"If you fall and hurt yourself in my shower I'll finish you off before you can sue me," she threatened sarcastically.

Quintin lowered the spoon and closed his eyes. He tried smiling, but could produce only a grimace. Opening his eyes, he stared at the angry expression on her face. "I won't fall," he said, raising the spoon and scooping up the oatmeal. He watched Victoria watching him. By the time he'd emptied the bowl her frown had disappeared.

Leaning over him, she took the tray. "Hurry up and get better, Quintin. I'm not very good at playing Florence Nightingale. I'm a chef not a nurse," she snapped, fighting her growing attraction for him.

He stared at her mouth, recalling its soft sweetness and the nectar he had tasted over and over. He loved her mouth; he loved her perfect little body, and he was in love with Victoria Jones.

His mind clear for the first time in hours, he quickly calculated what he needed to do to make Victoria his.

"I'm sorry," he apologized, and fell back on the pillows. Sighing, he turned his face away from her, closing his eyes.

Victoria felt properly chastised. She hadn't meant to snap at him. Oral surgery was not something any person welcomed. But she couldn't help her responses or her unexplained hostility. Quintin Lord was in her house, in her bed, and she didn't want him in either place. Or did she?

Feelings she felt long dead were back. After her divorce she refused to date, concentrating instead on her new career. Only Masud had been able to penetrate the shield she'd erected, but once the summer ended and she left Paris, the shield was back in place.

She had dated occasionally while she worked in Washington, D.C., but she never permitted the relationships to develop to a point where there would be talk of marriage or babies.

Victoria didn't mind a relationship—one that would remain platonic. She wanted Quintin Lord as her neighbor, not as her lover.

She sat down on the side of the bed. "I'm the one who should apologize, Quintin." She didn't see him smile. Patting his bare shoulder, she said, "I'll get all the things you'll need to shave."

Quintin waited for Victoria to leave, then, on shaking legs and wobbly knees, made his way into her bathroom. Bracing his back against a wall, he managed to shower and wash his hair without falling. Wrapping a towel around his waist, he returned to the bedroom, noting that Victoria had made the bed. She had turned back the sheets and laid out a change of clothes for him. His shaving equipment was on the bedside table.

He needed her and she had come. She had comforted him and given him sustenance, and she had done it because he was her neighbor.

He recalled Victoria's statement when he asked what she was offering. *What any other neighbor would offer, Mr. Lord. A cup of sugar, picking up your newspaper or mail when you're on vacation, and perhaps bringing you a cup of hot tea if you're down with the flu.*

Dressing slowly, Quintin's thoughts were filled with Victoria Jones. She had admonished him about his music and the untidiness of his apartment while she teased, flirted, and seduced him. She was a beautiful and enchanting enigma he wanted to make his own.

Victoria had recovered from the startling realization that she was inexorably drawn to her neighbor by the time she reentered the bedroom. Quintin lay on the bed, wearing a T-shirt and jeans, his bare feet crossed at the ankles, reading one of the Walter Mosley's Easy Rawlings mysteries she had left on the table next to the love seat.

He glanced up from the book, the fingers of his right hand going to his cheek. "Do you mind if I finish this chapter before you shave me?" Quintin asked through clenched teeth.

She swallowed hard and met his bold stare. He was pushing it.

"But you said you'd help me, Vicky." His voice was low, his expression contrite.

She didn't know whether to scream at Quintin or turn on her heel and walk out of the room. Having a wisdom tooth removed should not have rendered him an invalid.

Folding her hands on her narrow hips, Victoria sauntered over to the bed. "What else do you want me to do for you?"

Quintin closed the book and placed it on the bed. Exhaling heavily, he closed his eyes. If it wouldn't hurt so much he would've roared with laughter. She was on to him.

"It's not what I want you to do for me. It's what I want you to make for me."

She stood over him, staring down at his handsome face. "What?"

He reopened his eyes. There was just a hint of a smile inching the corners of her mouth upward. "Brownies. Double fudge chocolate, please."

"With or without the walnuts?"

"No nuts, please. Remember, I can't chew."

Victoria pushed her right fist under his nose. "You may not have a choice, neighbor, because I'm ready to feed you a knuckle sandwich."

Quintin reached for her hand and placed it along his swollen jaw. The silken skin on the back of her hand grazed the stubble of hair on his cheek.

Closing his eyes, he inhaled the haunting, cloying fragrance of the perfume on her wrist. His fingers tightened gently on her hand as he pulled her closer, losing himself in her delicate, feminine warmth.

He was floating again, this time without the aid of the painkiller. The images he had glimpsed in his dreams sprang to life.

Effortlessly, he pulled Victoria up over his body until her breasts were molded to the solid hardness of his chest. She lay rigid, her cheek pressed to his throat. Counting off the seconds, Quintin waited for her to relax before she sank into the cushioning of his protective embrace.

"Quin-tin?" His name came out low and hesitant.

His left arm moved from her waist to her shoulders, making her his captive. When his left hand cupped the back of her head, the gesture elicited a soft sigh of pleasure from her parted lips.

"I just want to hold you, Vicky."

And I don't want you to let me go, Victoria replied silently.

She wanted Quintin to hold her. The warmth of his arms was so masculine, so comforting. And it had been a man's protection that she missed most of all.

She had learned her assertiveness and independence from her mother, but Marion Jones had constantly reminded her daughters that there were times when a woman needed protection only a man could offer.

Marion's advice was manifested during the ten weeks Victoria lived in France completing her graduate studies.

Having Masud as her companion thwarted the advances of other men and permitted her to feel completely safe.

"Vicky," he moaned against her hair. He was in pain. His jaw ached and his heart bled. His craving for Victoria Jones had surpassed his craving for sailing. He desired her body but he wanted the whole woman more. Her warmth, fragrance, and her soft curves enveloped him, and despite his claim that he didn't have to sleep with her, his own body hardened with desire.

Smoothly and unhurriedly, he eased her down to lie beside him, his breath coming quickly. "I need a pill," Quintin gasped. He had to rid himself of the pain in his jaw and the shadow of foreboding tightening the muscles in his chest; something told him that for the first time in his life he would not get what he wanted. Some unnamed emotion whispered that Victoria Jones was beyond his grasp.

Nine

Quintin stared up at Victoria through half-lowered eyelids, his chest rising and falling evenly. The pain medication was working slowly. Slowly enough for him to savor the pleasure of her shaving him.

He had been too shocked to protest when she had straddled his thighs and lathered his face with shaving cream. Her warning of "don't move and don't say a word" was heeded as he rested his back against the pillows and yielded to her gentle touch.

The three-day growth of whiskers itched unbearably, and he did not want to risk further discomfort by scratching his bruised and tender jaw. The only time he neglected to shave was during an extended sailing trip. A beard and a hat shielded his face from the damaging rays of the sun and the bite of saltwater.

He was sailing again, but this time without a boat, drifting into nothingness. The last thing he remembered before Morpheus claimed him was the pressure of Victoria's hips pressing intimately against his groin as she bit down on her lower lip in concentration; he remembered that and his own body's uncontrollable response.

Victoria's hands stilled, her body stiffening. Quintin was asleep but there was no way she could mistake the swelling pushing up against her buttocks. He was asleep while another part of his anatomy was awake and throbbing.

She had shaved him quickly, her hands steady, using

the skills she had acquired to bone meats and prepare intricate and elaborate pastries and desserts.

Wiping a tiny spot of cream from his chin, she slipped fluidly off his prone form. She had tried leaning over Quintin to shave him, but hadn't been able to find a comfortable position or angle. Exasperated, she straddled him, hoping he would be asleep before she finished.

Standing beside the bed, she surveyed her handiwork, then splashed a cooling astringent onto his chin and cheeks. The discoloration along his left jaw was darker and more pronounced, while the swelling did not appear as severe as it did earlier that morning.

Victoria examined the man sleeping in her bed, wondering what it was about him that drew her to him like a fragile moth to a hot flame.

Her attraction to Quintin Lord was swift and unexpected, so unlike the slow, simmering attraction she had had for her ex-husband.

She had grown up loving Richard Morgan. He and her brother were good friends, but it wasn't until she turned fifteen that Richard acknowledged her as a member of the opposite sex. Before that time she had been Nat's little sister. She accepted Richard's grandmother's engagement ring on her eighteenth birthday and they were married a week after she had turned twenty.

It had been a fairy-tale romance culminating in a fairy-tale wedding between the descendants of two of Washington's oldest black families.

It ended because Richard wanted children to carry on the Morgan name—his own flesh-and-blood children, and it was only then that she realized Richard had married her not because he loved her, but because she was the daughter of Ambassador William Jones. Richard had always been impressed with the number of foreign dignitaries who visited the Joneses' opulent D.C. residence for formal dinner parties.

Victoria wondered if Quintin wanted children. She also wondered if people who grew up in large families wanted large families of their own.

She surveyed his relaxed features, finding his face more boyish in sleep. The tiny lines around his intense, penetrating gold-brown eyes were missing. The grooves around his mouth that were so attractive whenever he smiled were barely perceptible; however, the silkiness of his neatly barbered mustache that failed to conceal the sensuousness of his lower lip was as hypnotizing in sleep as it was in wakefulness.

Leaning over, she pressed a gentle kiss to his mouth. "Feel better, sweetheart," she breathed into his mouth. Quintin stirred briefly, then settled back into sleep.

Victoria sat on the high stool in the kitchen, telephone receiver cradled between her chin and shoulder while she made notations on a pad balanced on her knees. A slight frown dotted her smooth forehead.

"Why are you being stubborn, Nat?"

She had been arguing with her brother about the menu for his in-laws' anniversary celebration.

"It's not me, Vicky. It's Christine who says she doesn't want anyone to go away hungry."

"Okay," Victoria conceded. "The meat dishes will include butterflied lamb, smoked and fresh hams, roast turkey, and roast beef."

She heard a loud sigh come through the line. She had mailed her brother and sister-in-law a sample menu of what she would prepare for the anniversary celebration, but Christine Jones had rejected it, ignoring Victoria's suggestion that a summer fête called for a menu of lighter fare—broiled meats and fish, vegetable salads, and fruity desserts.

"Thanks, Vicky. You've just saved my marriage."

"You spoil your wife, Nathaniel Jones," Victoria teased.

"That's because I love her," Nat said in an even tone.

There was a pregnant silence before Victoria spoke again. "I'm glad you do, Nat." She smiled. The most secure feeling in the world was loving and being loved.

Could she love Quintin Lord and have him love her back?

What was the matter with her? She didn't want to fall in love. Or did she?

"Love you a bunch," she said softly, then rang off.

"Vicky?" The raspy male voice broke into her thoughts, and the subject of those torturous thoughts stood at the entrance to the kitchen, leaning against the arched doorway.

Victoria surveyed his bare feet, faded jeans riding low on his slim hips, and the stark white T-shirt stretched across his broad chest.

She left the stool and moved fluidly to his side. Her arm went around his waist and she led him over to a large wrought-iron table with matching chairs with plump black-and-white striped back and seat cushions.

"How are you feeling?" Her warm breath washed over his ear after he was seated.

"Hungry," he growled with a smile.

Victoria stared at his hair, and for the first time she realized how black it was. A soft, glossy, tightly curled midnight black. "How old are you, Quintin?"

Raising his head, he looked up at her. "Thirty-seven," he said without hesitating. "Why?"

She shrugged a shoulder. "Just curious."

His gaze captured hers. "What else are you curious about?"

"Nothing else." Her voice was calm, gentle.

"I'm single," he continued as if she hadn't spoken. "I have no encumbrances from my past. No ex-wives or children."

"Do you want children?" She didn't know what made her ask the question.

He measured her with a cool, appraising look. "I never gave having children much thought in the past. But now I don't think I'd mind a little Lord or two underfoot."

She had her answer. He wanted children. Turning away, she returned to the cooking island, ladling a simmering portion of creamed broccoli soup into a bowl.

Quintin devoured two bowls of the flavorful soup, feeling stronger than he had in days. His gaze followed Victoria as she stood at a counter measuring ingredients into a large aluminum mixing bowl. Four smaller aluminum bowls were also lined up on the counter.

He moved from the table and stood beside her, watching as she strained a mixture she had heated into a small bowl.

Noting dishes filled with ground pistachio nuts and coconut, he asked, "What are you making?"

"Gelato."

Quintin moved closer, his chest brushing her shoulder. "What is gelato?"

Victoria smiled up at him. "Italian ice cream."

"An Italian ice?"

"No, a cream. It's made with a custard base. When you add ingredients like espresso beans, hazelnut-and-chocolate candies, fresh coconut, or mascarpone cheese the result is an intense flavor. Gelaterias are as popular in Italy as fast-food restaurants are in the States."

Arching his eyebrows, Quintin gave her an expectant look. "Can I sample it?"

He reminded her of a little child who couldn't wait for his mother to finish with the cake batter so he could lick the mixing bowl.

"What flavor do you want?"

His eyes widened. "I have a choice?"

She laughed. "Yes, you have a choice."

"Vanilla."

"Vanilla," she repeated. "Can't you come up a flavor that's not so conservative?"

"But I am conservative, Victoria," he protested.

She patted his chest. "Not quite, Quintin Lord. Not with both of your ears pierced."

His hand went to the small gold hoop in his right ear. "You don't like the earrings?"

Victoria wanted to say she liked the earrings in his ears; she liked his hair, his eyes, mouth, and she liked everything that made Quintin Lord the man he was.

He looked at her as if he were photographing her with his eyes, and the smoldering flame she saw in his gaze startled her. Unconsciously, she moved closer to him, both palms flattened on his solid chest.

A soft, mysterious smile tilted her mouth upward. "I like your earrings very much," she replied softly.

Quintin folded her in a protective embrace, his fingers splayed over her back. His heart was a low, steady pumping. Her arms slipped up and circled his strong neck, bringing her even closer.

He swayed slightly and Victoria pulled back. "Sit down before you fall down," she ordered in a quiet voice.

Quintin obeyed. He wasn't going to fall down. What he wanted to do was fall into bed with Victoria and stay there for the rest of his life. He wanted to hold her, kiss her, and brand her with the love he had never offered another woman.

Victoria removed a plastic container from the commercial walk-in freezer and scooped out a serving of mascarpone gelato. She poured a cup of hot espresso over the scoop, then placed the dish in front of Quintin.

"Mascarpone gelato served *affogato.*"

Picking up a spoon, Quintin swallowed a portion of the frozen Italian cream cheese drowned in espresso coffee.

His hand halted and he stared across the table at Victoria as she sat down with her own dish of gelato.

Registering his startled expression, she smiled. "Exquisite, isn't it?"

Nodding his head in stunned silence, Quintin returned her smile. Within minutes he finished the mascarpone gelato and extended the empty dish. "More."

"Keep eating and you're going to get fat," Victoria warned, picking up his dish.

"I'll jog longer," he replied, licking the spoon.

She served him another flavor, blood orange, the taste reminiscent of a Creamsicle. Quintin took his time eating this one, savoring the taste of creamy sweet red oranges.

Victoria was pleased with Quintin's reaction to the gelato. She intended to introduce the dazzling popular Italian dessert to her new clients.

"What others flavors have you created?" he asked after he finished his second serving.

"Ricotta, banana, lemon, apricot, espresso, chocolate varieties, ginger, and a very wicked zabaglione. I usually make the fruit varieties when they are in season."

"What is zabaglione?"

"It's made with marsala wine, egg yolks and sugar," she explained. "It can be served as a sauce, dessert, or a beverage."

Quintin smiled. "It sounds wickedly rich and fattening."

"What it can be is wickedly potent."

Like you, Quintin mused. Delicate, beautiful, and potent.

Rising to his feet, he stared down at Victoria. "I think I've intruded on your hospitality long enough. I'd better be getting back to my place."

Victoria rose with him. It seemed strange to her that, just a few hours ago she couldn't wait for him to go home. She realized the more time she spent with Quintin the more she liked him. But she didn't want to get too used to his company; she didn't want to need him.

"I'll check on you later," she promised.

Quintin gave her a long, penetrating look, then flashed a shy smile. "You won't have to check in on me. I'll be back for my double fudge chocolate brownies," he said, wiggling his eyebrows. "Without the nuts, please," he added as Victoria folded her hands on both hips.

She stuck her tongue out at him and he blew her a kiss, prompting a smile from her. When he left her apartment she was still smiling. Wrapping her arms around her body, she closed her eyes and swayed sensuously to a tune in her head, not realizing it was the Anita Baker hit "Just Because."

Ten

Quintin climbed the staircase to his bedroom and sat on the bed. The telephone answering machine on the end table registered four calls. Pushing a button, he listened to the recorded messages: one from his mother, two from his sister Sharon, and one from Ethan Bennington.

He returned the calls, reassuring Etta Mae Lord he would not miss the family's Memorial Day celebration. He smiled after hanging up because for as long as he could remember since he turned twenty-five he was reminded to bring a young lady with him. His mother had become relentless about his marrying and adding to her growing number of grandchildren.

The call to Sharon allayed her fears that he had not succumbed to complications brought on by the oral surgery. She laughed nervously after he teased her, then reported Hannibal was well and didn't seem to miss him very much. He told her he would pick the schnauzer up in a few days and rang off.

The return call to Ethan proved puzzling. "I've got some good news, but I think I'd rather tell you in person," Ethan stated. "Are you going to be home tonight?"

Quintin touched his swollen jaw. "I'll be here, buddy."

"I'll see you in twenty minutes."

Quintin hung up, wondering about Ethan Bennington's good news. Ethan was the director of a Baltimore cultural center that established the criteria for recreation and community centers throughout the Baltimore metropolitan area.

The two men had met four years ago at a city-wide cultural exposition. Ethan had displayed several antique pieces from his private collection of furnishings dating back to seventeenth and eighteenth-century colonial America, while Quintin showcased his coveted daguerreotypes and prints of black army regiments from the Civil War through World War II. What had begun as an interest in each other's passion for art turned quickly into a friendship of mutual admiration and respect.

Staring down at his bare feet, Quintin remembered he had left his shoes in Victoria's bedroom. His eyes lit up as he remembered bits and pieces of the last twenty-four hours: Victoria caring for him—her gentleness and her annoyance whenever he tested her patience.

He loved the way her eyes narrowed as she faced him down and the soft, sweet scent of her body. He loved everything about her. He was deeply and inexorably in love with his neighbor.

Ethan Powell Bennington's generous mouth opened and closed several times before he whispered, "What happened?"

"Wisdom tooth," Quintin replied, opening the door wider and stepping aside to let Ethan into the entryway.

Staring back at Quintin, Ethan let out an audible whistle. "It looks as if you ran into a roundhouse right."

I'd be willing to run into a roundhouse right if only to have Victoria Jones nurse me back to health, he thought.

Ethan walked into the living room, stopping short. "What happened to the clutter?"

"Cleaning woman," Quintin explained.

Ethan gave him a skeptical look. "I can remember the

time I offered you a gift of a cleaning service and you turned it down. What brought this on?"

"I wanted to impress a young lady," Quintin replied candidly.

"Do I know her?"

"No."

"Then she must be special."

Quintin managed what could be called a smile. "She's very special," he confirmed.

Ethan clamped a well-groomed hand on Quintin's shoulder. "There's hope for you yet. When will I meet her?"

"Soon enough. Can I get you something to drink?"

Ethan stared at Quintin, smiling widely. "I'll have a brandy." He walked over to the sliding-glass doors leading to the patio and stepped out into the warm twilight. Within minutes Quintin handed him a snifter of premium French brandy. "Where's yours?" he asked, noting the one glass.

Quintin folded his body down to a rattan chair. "I'll pass. I'm taking a painkiller."

Ethan took a matching chair, then took a sip of the brandy, his eyes narrowing as he stared over the rim at Quintin. Placing the glass on a low table, he crossed an ankle over a knee.

"I'd like to ask a favor of you, Quintin."

"All you have to do is ask, buddy."

Ethan turned away, and the waning light softened the distinct outline of his patrician features. Ethan Powell Bennington exemplified breeding and wealth, and as a result of those qualities he had become a most eligible bachelor among Baltimore's social elite.

"I've asked my sister to handle Ryan's adoption, and when it's finalized I want you to be his godfather," he stated quietly.

If Quintin hadn't known how serious Ethan was about the young boy who'd spent most of his ten years in foster and group homes he would have laughed at his friend. But he didn't.

"I'd be honored, Ethan," he replied without hesitating.

Turning, Ethan extended his hand, grinning broadly. "Thanks, buddy."

Quintin took the proffered hand, pumping It. "When do you expect everything to be finalized?"

"Caroline's hoping it will not take more than six months. I'd like to be able to take 'my son' home for good before Christmas."

"I'm certain Ryan is as anxious to have you for a father as you are to have him as your son," Quintin replied.

Ethan let out his breath slowly, closing his eyes. The anxiety he had felt for months had begun to subside. His wish was about to come true—even if he had to wait another six months.

Having disclosed his good news, Ethan and Quintin talked for an hour, discussing the upcoming plans for the cultural center's fifth anniversary.

Quintin promised he would supervise the set decoration project the art students planned for the drama club skit. He had become a volunteer when he offered to teach an art history course twice each month during the school year; once he convinced the young children that a nude statue or model was art and not pornography he was able to open their young minds to a world where art told the history before many cultures had a written language.

Night had fallen as Ethan prepared to leave. "Ryan keeps asking when you're going to take him out on your boat."

Quintin winced. He should've known better than to promise the child and not deliver. He knew it had to be soon because he was scheduled to begin a shoot in two weeks.

"If you're free next Saturday and if the weather holds we can go out a few miles."

He had planned to sail down to the Keys with Victoria, but knew that was now impossible because he had to return to the oral surgeon late Friday afternoon.

"You're on, Quintin."

Ethan thanked him again, then left for his two-bedroom cottage in a Baltimore suburb across town.

Quintin returned to sit on the patio, watching the clear nighttime sky and registering the differing sounds of chirping crickets and the noisy buzzing of cicadas. The golden glow of light spilled out onto the concrete floor of the neighboring patio. Only a wrought-iron railing separated the two residences.

"Vicky," he whispered. As if she had heard him the sliding-glass doors opened and she stepped out into the warm night.

He didn't move, blending into the shadows and watching her as she moved fluidly to the railing and peered out in the direction of the tiny lights surrounding the Olympic-size swimming pool belonging to the residents of the duplex units.

She had changed from her jeans and T-shirt to a light-colored gauzy dress that left her shoulders bare. The bodice crisscrossed her breasts and skimmed her tiny waist before flowing out around her calves.

Quintin was stunned, unable to move or breathe. His lungs burned and nearly exploded before he exhaled and melted back against the hard rattan of his chair. Every line of her body was revealed in the diffused light—the curve of her waist, the roundness of her hips, and the slim length of her thighs and legs.

Her hair was pulled back and secured in a twist, allowing him an unobscured view of her lovely face. He didn't know how long he watched her, but even after Victoria had turned and reentered her apartment he continued to see her.

Double fudge chocolate brownies forgotten, Quintin returned to his living room and picked up a sketch pad. Within minutes the image of the vision imprinted on his brain came to life. He worked for hours, sketching and erasing before the likeness of Victoria Jones came alive on the large sheet of paper.

Streaks of dawn had pierced the nighttime sky when Quintin finally made his way up the staircase to his bed. He slept deeply, only waking to the chiming of the doorbell.

Victoria listened for a sound of movement, then rang again. Quintin hadn't returned for his brownies the night before and she thought maybe he had forgotten about them. She had shrugged it off until the thought that perhaps he had fallen and injured himself startled her out of sleep. Tossing restlessly until the sky lightened with the dawn of a new day, she showered, dressed, and went to seek out her neighbor.

His door opened without her knocking, and she stared up at a blurry-eyed Quintin Lord. "Good morning," she said cheerfully.

Quintin ran a hand over his hair. "Good morning," he mumbled back.

Trying to appear nonplussed at seeing his half-clothed body, she shrugged her shoulders. "Just checking to see that you're okay." She pulled her gaze away from the jeans he had slipped on. He had zipped them but hadn't bothered to snap the waistband. His belly was flat with corded muscles visible under the feathering of coarse hair disappearing under the denim fabric.

"I'm fine," he said, covering his mouth and a yawn.

She handed him a small shopping bag containing his deck shoes, shaving equipment, and the bottle of pain medication.

"Breakfast will be ready in half an hour. If you're not ready I'll leave it outside your door."

"I'll be ready," he grunted, taking the bag. He waited until she returned to her apartment before he closed the door.

Seeing her again, up close, confirmed that he had captured a remarkable likeness when he had sketched her. He only had to modify the slight tilt of her chin whenever she glanced up at him and soften the curve of her lower lip before he transferred the sketch to a canvas and completed it with vibrant oils.

He had already thought of a name for his masterpiece. "Night Magic."

Quintin sat opposite Victoria at the table on her patio. He had surprised her by stepping over the railing separating the two patios, seating her after she had set the table.

A cooling breeze lifted her unbound hair around her face. This morning she had worn a bang swept across her forehead, the back and sides curving loosely under her chin and along her nape.

Her gaze swept slowly over his face. "Your jaw is looking a lot better this morning."

Quintin nodded. "Much of the swelling is gone, but the bruise looks hideous."

Victoria uncovered a dish of steaming-hot grits. "Even with the bruise you can still turn a few heads, Adonis," she teased, spooning a portion of the grits onto a plate. She uncovered another dish with fluffy yellow scrambled eggs.

Leaning back on his chair, Quintin smiled. "It sort of gives me a rugged look, don't you think?"

"It looks as if someone rocked your chops."

"Some doctor named Pearson did," he replied, his eyes crinkling in amusement.

"Remind me to kiss it later and make it all better."

"I'm going to hold you to that promise, missy." He gave her a sensual smile, filling his own plate with grits, eggs, and creamy butter.

Quintin downed the grits, eggs, a serving of applesauce, and two cups of coffee, then leaned over the table, asking, "Where are my double fudge chocolate brownies?"

Victoria bit down on her lower lip, smiling. "Where do you put all of your food? You should weigh at least two hundred pounds."

"I'm not far from it. I weigh in at one eighty-six."

His weight was deceiving. She thought he'd weighed between one hundred seventy and seventy-five. No wonder she could hardly move him.

"I see why you jog," she replied.

"Do you want to walk tomorrow morning?"

"Before or after breakfast?"

"Before, of course," he said.

Raising her chin, Victoria nodded. "Okay."

"Seven," she confirmed.

Quintin caught her gaze and held it, noting the shape of her eyes, the curve of her cheekbones, and the fullness of her soft sensual mouth. Victoria Jones had the sexiest mouth of any woman he had ever kissed.

"I'm afraid there's going to be a change of plans for next weekend."

Victoria gave him a puzzled look. "What's next weekend?"

"Our excursion to the Keys. We're going to have to put it off until another time."

"That's all right, Quintin."

"There will be another time, Vicky." She smiled demurely, lowering her gaze. "But the weekend doesn't have to be a complete waste," he continued. "I'm planning to take *Jamila* out on Saturday. I've invited a good friend and his son, if that's all right with you." But before she could reply he added, "Why don't you invite a friend or two, then we can have a pre-Memorial Day celebration."

"How large is *Jamila?*"

"Large enough. It sleeps four and the deck can easily accommodate twelve."

Victoria filled her cup with coffee. "Where did you come up with the name *Jamila?*" She wondered if he had named it after a girlfriend.

"It took months before I found just the right name. I finally found it in a book of baby names. It's from Somalia and it means 'beautiful'." He didn't say that if he had to come up with a name for it now it would be Victoria.

"You remind me of a modern-day Paul Gauguin. I can imagine you sailing to a tropical island where you'd spend the rest of your life painting and drinking coconut milk."

"I've seriously thought about it."

Leaning forward, Victoria studied his solemn expression. "Do you ever think you'd leave Baltimore?"

"Maybe one day." He shook his head slowly. "But not now."

Her heart pounded an erratic rhythm. She was venturing into dangerous territory with her line of questioning. What did she want from Quintin? What did she want for herself?

"Why not now, Quintin?"

Because of you, Vicky, his head screamed. Because there would be no way that he could leave her. Not now. He loved her. Didn't she know—couldn't she tell that he loved her? Didn't she realize he was going just a little crazy because he had never been in love before.

"I've met someone . . ." he began.

Victoria felt as if he had knifed her. There was no reason for the pain, but she felt it as surely as if he'd picked up the knife on the table and driven it into her heart.

"A woman?" she asked hoarsely.

"Yes, Vicky."

A bitter jealousy stirred inside her. Suddenly she hated the tall, graceful woman she had seen leaving his apartment.

"She's a lucky woman," she said in a quiet whisper.

Quintin's grin was slow in coming. "I'd like to think she is. However, I think I'm the one with all of the luck."

Victoria finished her coffee, then rose to her feet. "I'd better get your brownies before you haunt me."

She made her way back into the house, Quintin's low chuckle of laughter following her. It wasn't until she reached the kitchen that she felt the prickle of tears behind her eyelids. She had been deceiving herself. She was falling in love with her neighbor.

But it was all for nothing because he was in love with another woman. Why did she always pick the wrong man to fall in love with?

First Richard and now Quintin. She might be older now, but she certainly wasn't any wiser.

Eleven

Quintin followed Victoria into the kitchen, watching as she placed moist brownie squares in a colorful plastic container and covered it. He also noted several large trays filled with fried crab cakes. Two other trays were filled with potato salad. An industrial roll of colorful plastic wrap rested beside the trays.

Quintin's eyes glittered with amusement. "How about I sample the crab cakes and potato salad to see if they're good," he drawled, reaching for the trays.

Moving closer to him, Victoria slapped at his right hand. "Don't you dare touch that! I left some out for you."

He affected a pout. "Where are you taking those?"

"These are going to church for . . ." She broke off, hands on both hips. "Wait just a minute, Mr. Lord. Before I moved in here you existed on greasy, additive-filled, artery-clogging swill and now I can't prepare a crouton without you wanting to sample a crumb."

Quintin reached for Victoria, molding her feminine curves to his length. "You've spoiled me," he crooned, smiling down at her upturned face.

Victoria's gaze caressed his features, lingering on the sweeping arch of his thick black eyebrows, the tiny lines around his large laughing eyes and the sensual curve of his masculine mouth.

"I'm considering unspoiling you," she teased.

"Too late." His head lowered and he nuzzled her neck.

"I'll move away," she continued, her voice low and halting as his mouth moved slowly over her hair.

"I'll follow you, Vicky. I'll sail the world searching for you."

Her arms going around his slim waist, Victoria melted against his body, luxuriating in the unyielding strength that was Quintin Lord's.

She wanted the man! She wanted him more than she had ever wanted Richard. She wanted to know what it was about Quintin Lord that drew her to him.

Closing her eyes, she gave in to the powerful passions coursing throughout her as Quintin sculpted her body with his fingers. He was the artist, the sculptor molding and shaping her to his will.

Quintin was certain Victoria could feel his trembling, his tentativeness. He wanted and needed her so badly he was lightheaded. Victoria Jones filled his every waking and sleeping moment. She had possessed him and controlled him.

"Quintin." His name was a strangled cry. He moaned in response, his hands busy cupping her hips and pressing her to his heated groin.

"Quintin," she repeated.

His breathing was heavy and ragged. "Don't move—not yet," he pleaded. He wanted her to know that she aroused him—that she had the power to turn him into a weak-kneed trembling mass of uncontrollable passion.

Victoria felt his maleness surging against her thighs. She felt the tension turning his muscles into bands of steel. She was experienced enough to know that the moment of sexual sparring had evolved beyond their control. All that was needed was a blink, an intake of breath, or a spark before they dissolved into a precious and profound oneness.

"I need you, Vicky," he murmured against her ear.

She stiffened. She didn't want him to need her; she

wanted him to *want* her. Richard needed her, and not once had he ever said that he wanted her. If she was going to become involved with Quintin it had to be because they both wanted each other.

"Let me go, Quintin."

"Vicky."

She pushed against his solid chest. "I said, let me go!" This time her tone was layered with a chilly warning.

He released her, stepping back and staring down at the set of her mouth. Victoria Jones was upset. But what had he done? He had only told her the truth.

Turning away, Victoria picked up the box of plastic wrap. "I'll see you later."

Quintin watched as she pulled out enough rose-colored plastic to cover a tray of potato salad, then he turned and silently made his way out of her kitchen. Returning to his own living room, he flopped down on a dark-brown leather chair and cradled his face in his palms.

Had he moved too quickly? Had he assumed she would fall into bed with him because she had allowed him to kiss her? Lowering his hands, Quintin stared at the screen he used as a backdrop for a photography shoot.

He had to remind himself that Victoria Jones was different. Different from any other woman he had ever met. He couldn't rush her into bed.

A wry smile curved his mouth. He would wait her out. She wasn't going anywhere and neither was he.

Victoria directed the four young men to her van and watched as they unloaded the trays of crab cakes and potato salad. Her housewarming celebration had borne fruit. One of her friends had called frantically the night before with an announcement that her grandmother's arthritis was acting up and the elderly woman couldn't prepare the crab cakes and potato salad she had promised for her church's revival festivities.

Victoria had checked her inventory on the computer that rested on a counter in the kitchen, sighing in relief. She had had enough lump crabmeat and potatoes on hand to fulfill the request. It had taken her a long time to set up the disk listing the items, quantity, and the purchase date, but it had proven invaluable. Within minutes she knew whether she could prepare any dish on very short notice.

"Thanks, Victoria, for helping out my grandmother," Nadine Erskine said, smiling broadly. "Grandmama never would've been able to hold her head up again if Sister Sara started gossip saying that she used her arthritis as an excuse not to make her special dishes. There's been an ongoing feud between my grandmother and Sister Sara Barnes for years. Sister Sara claims no one can make crab cakes or potato salad the way she does."

Victoria laughed. "But is Sister Sara good?"

Nadine nodded. "She's good, but not as good as my grandmother. The only one I know who can make better potato salad is you," she stated, handing Victoria a check.

"Then tell your grandmother not to tell anyone that I prepared the salad if she wants to keep her reputation." Victoria took the check, slipping it into her blouse pocket.

"I would, but I can't count on Grandmama. She'll probably sing your praises to the top of the tent, and after that you won't be able to keep up with the orders that'll come your way. These ladies can be so competitive."

"Well, I can't say I won't appreciate the business," Victoria remarked. She reached into the van and withdrew a decorative black-and-white striped shopping bag with VJ Catering and her telephone number inscribed in black script along each white stripe. "This is a little something for you, Nadine."

Nadine took the bag, peering down at its contents. "What is it?"

"Vanilla and chocolate wafer points and an Italian ice cream. Keep the ice cream frozen until you're ready to eat it. Then you should soften it slightly in the refrigerator before serving it."

Holding the bag in one hand, Nadine threw her arms around Victoria. "Thanks, girlfriend. For helping my grandmother and for the goodies."

"Anytime." She hugged Nadine back.

She returned to her vehicle and backed out of the parking lot. The lot was filling up quickly with people who had come to the large Baptist church for their week-long revival marathon. The program had listed popular evangelists as well as unlimited food for all who came to praise the Lord while testifying to His good works.

Victoria drove through downtown Baltimore, finding it hard to believe that it had been just two days since she picked up Quintin from the oral surgeon. He had spent only a day in her apartment but it could have been a week. Her emotions went into double overtime whenever she was with him. What was there about the man that wouldn't allow her to keep her balance?

There was one thing she was certain of concerning Quintin. She was never bored with him.

Victoria slid back the sliding screen door and stepped out onto the patio. She made her way to a chaise longue and picked up the Sunday newspaper. She'd planned to spend the afternoon reading the paper and relaxing.

An hour later it was the ringing of the cordless telephone on a wrought-iron table that pulled Victoria out of sleep. She had dozed off.

Sitting upright, she reached for the receiver, hesitating

when she saw Quintin reclining on a matching chaise less than three feet away from her.

"What are you doing here?" Her voice was heavy with sleep.

Quintin pointed to the ringing telephone. "Answer the phone, Vicky."

Victoria snatched up the receiver. "Hello."

"Who set you off, Vicky?" asked a familiar female voice.

"I'm sorry, Jo." Victoria lowered her voice to keep a grinning Quintin from overhearing her conversation. "Something just startled me." She saw Quintin frown when she referred to him as *something.* "What's up?"

"What are you doing next Saturday?"

Victoria remembered she had promised Quintin she would go out on his boat with him. "I'm invited to go sailing," she informed Joanna. "What did you have in mind?"

There came a loud sigh through the wire. "Nothing as exciting as a sailing expedition."

"How would you like to come along?"

"Are you sure?" Joanna questioned.

"Of course I'm sure, Jo. I was told I could invite a friend." Quintin's frown deepened further with the mention of 'friend.' "We'll be leaving early Saturday morning, so why don't you stay over Friday night."

"You're on. I'll call you before Friday and let you know what time to expect me."

"Good. I'll talk to you later."

Victoria returned the phone to its cradle, smiling. "I've invited a friend for Saturday."

"So I heard," Quintin mumbled angrily.

Why the hell did he have to open his big mouth and tell Victoria that she could invite a friend? Now he was going to have to call on all of his self-control not to snap this Joe's neck if the man . . .

He groaned inwardly. Tossing Joe overboard on Saturday would be too late. The man was going to stay with Victoria Friday night.

Quintin couldn't clench his teeth without experiencing discomfort so he reclined on the chaise, closing his eyes.

Getting next to Victoria Jones was as difficult as trying to pick fleas off a dog's back. He had to come up with a way to win her love.

Victoria assumed a similar position on her chaise, also closing her eyes. "Is there something you wanted, Quintin?" she asked in a lazy tone.

Yes, there is, Quintin thought. He wanted her to be his wife and the mother of his children. A fist of shock squeezed his heart before letting go. How had it happened? How had he so quickly, deeply, fallen in love with Victoria? "I want my brownies," he said instead.

She sat up quickly, staring at him. "Why didn't you take them this morning?"

Quintin didn't move or open his eyes. "You threw me out before I could."

She folded her hands on her hips. "I didn't throw you out."

"You said 'I'll see you later.' I took that to mean I was dismissed."

Swinging her legs off the chaise, Victoria stood up and glared at him. "You and those damned brownies!"

"For shame, Vicky. Swear words on Sunday," he teased.

Victoria went into the house, cursing the man in English and in French.

Twelve

After walking with Quintin Monday morning Victoria did not see him again until early Saturday, and it wasn't until he pounded on her door and she opened it to see him standing there did she realize how much she had missed him.

"What are you trying to do, wake the dead, Quintin Lord?"

"We're supposed to cast off at sunrise, matey," he said with a wide grin.

She couldn't help smiling back at him. The bruising and swelling along his jaw had disappeared, no longer marring the face she had grown to love. Yes, she could admit that to herself. He loved another woman, yet she was in love with Quintin Lord. It had taken time away from him to realize that she wanted and loved him.

She loved his masculinity, his teasing nature, and his creative brilliance. And she also had come to realize that he was so easy to love. There was nothing complicated about the man.

He was dressed in white: shorts, T-shirt, and deck shoes, and his sherry-colored gaze swept quickly over her attire of tan walking shorts, orange T-shirt, and matching orange Bass canvas shoes. The tan painter's cap on her head would protect her face from the hot sun.

Victoria opened the door wider. "The food chest is in the kitchen."

"I didn't ask you to cook," he said, smiling down at her lovely face. "I'd planned for us to dock somewhere and pick up lunch."

She patted his muscular shoulder. "My treat."

Leaning over, he raised her chin and placed a light kiss on her mouth. Thanks, Vicky."

Joanna Landesmann walked into the entryway the moment Quintin kissed Victoria. She stopped short, watching his fingers curve gently around her friend's upper arms. Then, without warning, Victoria was in his arms, her body molded intimately to his. Retreating quietly, Joanna went back to the kitchen, her face mirroring the satisfied grin of a cat who had just devoured a dish of sweet cream.

Quintin deepened the kiss, his tongue searching the warm softness of her mouth. Her lips parted, delighting him as her tongue met his in an intimate heated joining.

Again he had stayed away from Victoria Jones, but to no avail. His desire for her had not waned nor had his love diminished. What he felt for her was real—real and passionate, and it wasn't until he'd been away from her for two days that he realized he was jealous. Insanely jealous of this Joe she had invited to stay with her. This Joe she had invited to sail on *Jamila.*

Well, if Joe wanted Victoria Jones he had to come through Quintin Lord, because he had no intention of losing her. Besides—what the hell kind of name was Joe? Joseph or Joel maybe, but not plain old run-of-the-mill Joe.

Victoria curved her arms under Quintin's and clung to his shoulders, abandoning herself to the whirl of sensations gripping her mind and body.

He devoured her mouth and she returned his hunger with a similar passion. "Quintin," she murmured, trying to catch her breath.

Pulling back, he registered the startled look in her large dark eyes. "You were past due on your payments for the watercolor, Vicky. I decided to collect the late charges." He swept the hat from her head and buried his face in her hair.

Victoria rested her forehead against his chest, holding back laughter. "You didn't say anything about late charges or interest."

His hands were busy caressing her back. "You didn't read the fine print, Miss Jones."

"What other hidden charges did I miss?"

Holding her at arm's length, he studied her face thoughtfully. "There's one more, but I can't reveal it at this time."

"I'm going to report you to the state's attorney general for fraudulent business practices, Mr. Lord," she teased.

He smiled. "Lawsuits are known to take years to settle."

"I have time, Quintin."

His smile faded as a serious light filled his gaze. "So do I, honey. I have nothing but time."

Victoria knew his statement held a double meaning.

"What time are we sailing?"

They sprang apart at the sound of Joanna's voice. Quintin stared numbly at the woman with short red hair.

"Do you remember my friend, Jo Landesmann?" Victoria asked.

Quintin managed several croaking sounds until he recovered. Joe was not a Joe but a *Jo.* "Of course," he said, extending his hand. He was certain both women heard his sigh of relief.

Jo took the proffered hand, drinking in his sensual smile. He was more than gorgeous. He was magnificent.

"I'm ready to ship out, Quintin," Jo replied, finding her own voice.

Unlike Victoria and Quintin, Joanna wore a pair of white cotton slacks and a long-sleeved cotton gauze navy-blue shirt. She had learned not to expose her fair skin to the sun.

Jo pointed to a large canvas bag near the door. "That's also going aboard."

Quintin looked from the bag and back to Jo, then to Victoria. "What on earth are you two taking along? I invite a couple of guys and they bring what they have on their backs. Meanwhile, you ladies bring everything including your vanity mirrors. Out on the sea we usually rough it."

Victoria smoothed back her hair, then replaced her cap. "Just take it, please," she drawled in a bored tone.

Quintin held out his hand. "Give me your keys, Vicky. You and Jo wait outside while I bring everything out and lock up here."

As if they'd rehearsed it, Victoria and Joanna saluted Quintin. "Aye, aye, sir."

The two women waited until they were outside and seated in Quintin's four-wheeler before collapsing in hysterical laughter.

"Did you . . . did you . . . see . . . see his face when I pointed to the bag?" Jo sputtered.

"Yes-ss," Victoria hiccuped. "Here he comes," she whispered as Quintin came down the front stairs with the bag atop the chest. Hannibal bounded down behind him and waited patiently at the curb while Quintin opened the tailgate. He secured the chest and bag, then lifted Hannibal into the cargo area and secured the tailgate door.

Walking around to the passenger side of the vehicle, he opened the door. Motioning with his hand, Quintin ordered, "Vicky, you ride up front with me."

Before she could reply, he pulled her from her seat and settled her in the one beside the driver. He slammed the door, glaring at her through the open window. His angry expression registered: *Don't start none—won't be none.*

Victoria glanced over her shoulder at Jo, but the redhead was busy crooning to Hannibal. Had she forced

Quintin to lose his temper? This was another side of him she had never seen.

Fifteen minutes later Quintin pulled up in front of a small cottage in a wealthy Baltimore suburb. A profusion of wildflowers surrounded the property enclosed by a white picket fence. At exactly six o'clock a man and a young boy emerged from the house.

"Take a look, ladies," Quintin said. "Two males and no bags," he taunted.

Victoria did not reply, but gave Quintin a smug smile. She intended to make him beg before she shared anything she and Jo brought along for the trip.

A light breeze ruffled the man's brown wavy hair, and as he neared the four-wheeler both Victoria and Jo were staring openly at him.

Quintin waited until the two were seated on the backseat beside Jo before he made the introductions. "Victoria Jones, Joanna Landesmann. Ethan Bennington and his son Ryan." There was a chorus of hellos and smiles.

Victoria longed to turn around and glance at Ethan Bennington and his son but quelled her curiosity. To use Jo's expression, the man was "gorgeous."

Ethan had what she thought of as classic good looks. His face was finely chiseled—each feature exquisitely defined and balanced. However, Ryan Bennington looked nothing like his father. Where Ethan was fair, Ryan was dark. The young boy's coloring was a rich mocha-brown, his black hair thick and tightly curling, while his features were indicative of his biracial heritage.

Ethan's hazel eyes swept over the cargo area. "I thought you weren't going to bring anything, Quintin."

Quintin glanced up at the rearview mirror. "I didn't. The booty belongs to the ladies." Ethan's gaze went from Jo to Victoria before he turned away, hiding a smile.

The gesture was not lost on Joanna and Victoria, and

they silently acknowledged that Ethan Bennington would also join Quintin as a beggar before the sun set.

Jo kept up a steady stream of conversation with Ryan, who after some urging revealed he was ten and had just completed a sixth-grade curriculum even though he was in the fifth grade.

All conversation came to an abrupt halt when Quintin parked and directed everyone to the slip where his *Jamila* was moored.

"Why didn't you tell me it was a yacht?" Jo whispered in Victoria's ear.

"He told me it was a cruiser," she whispered back.

"It's a *yacht,*" Jo insisted, staring at more than thirty-five feet of gleaming white hull.

Ryan was equally impressed as he stood on the pier, eyes wide and mouth gaping.

"It's all gassed up and ready to go, Mr. Lord," reported a wiry man. The network of fine lines on his tanned, leathery face was a testament of too much sun and salt water.

Quintin patted the man's back. "Thanks, Patrick."

"When can I expect you back, Mr. Lord?"

"Probably before sunset."

Patrick saluted. "Good sailing, folks."

Quintin helped Victoria, Jo, and Ryan up the ramp while Ethan carried the chest and the large canvas bag on board. Hannibal, as familiar with the deck of *Jamila* as he was with his home, made his way across the teakwood deck and settled down in a cool area under the pilothouse.

"Where do you want these?" Ethan asked, still holding the chest and bag.

"Both go in the galley," Victoria said, watching Quintin as he sat down on the deck and removed his shoes.

Standing and walking over to a closed compartment, he lifted the top of a chest and withdrew five life jackets.

Extending a bright yellow one to Ryan, he said, "Put this on."

Ryan stared at the jacket, pouting. "I can swim."

"So can I," Quintin retorted, "but I have a healthy respect for the ocean."

"Put it on, Ryan." Ethan's voice was soft, yet held a ring of authority that warned Ryan not to challenge him.

The boy took the jacket and slipped it on. His dark mood lifted slightly once he saw that all of the adults did not seem to mind that they had to wear the life jackets.

The rising sun was high in the late-spring sky when Quintin lifted the anchor and maneuvered the ship out of the harbor and into Chesapeake Bay.

Victoria stood at the railing with Jo, watching the fleet of boats in the harbor grow smaller, then disappear altogether. The feel of the rising and falling deck under her feet was hypnotic, and giving in to the urge she sat down and removed her shoes. The teak deck was soft as old suede, and warm from the sun.

I always wanted to be a part of a sailing expedition to Africa. She remembered Quintin's statement as she ran a hand over the smooth polished railing.

Shifting slightly, she stared up at Quintin as he stood in the pilothouse, bare feet slightly parted and sunglasses shielding his eyes from the rays of the bright sun glinting off the choppy water as he steered his beloved *Jamila* out into the Intercoastal Waterway.

Everything about him was confident and relaxed. He lived his life exactly the way he wanted to live it. He painted, sailed, and came and went at will.

She thought of his girlfriend, and wondered why Quintin hadn't invited her to sail with them. A wry smile curved her lips. She hoped the woman was worthy of Quintin's love.

Victoria was unaware that Jo had moved away to talk

to Ryan and that Quintin had taken her place at the rail until she heard, "Awesome, isn't it?"

Victoria jumped at the sound of the familiar voice. "Who's piloting—"

"Ethan took over," Quintin interrupted, staring down at her delicate profile. "Have you got your sea legs yet?"

She took a step back from the railing and rose on her toes, arms outstretched, and affected a second position ballet pose.

"Good enough, Captain Lord."

Quintin was transfixed by the graceful move, his gaze glued to her legs and the incredible arch of her bare feet. "Very good," he replied. Moving closer, he pulled her to his side, his right arm holding her captive. "When are you going to dance for me, Vicky?"

She felt her blood run cold. She would never dance again—not for Quintin and not for anyone.

"Never," she replied, pushing against his firm grip.

He wouldn't let her escape. "Why not?"

She didn't answer, her gaze fixed on the water.

Quintin saw a flicker of pain. It was the same pain he had noticed the first time she spoke of giving up dancing. "What made you give up your dance career? Maybe I should rephrase the question. Who made you give up your career?"

Victoria could have been carved out of marble as she stood at the railing, unmoving. "It wasn't who or what, Quintin. It was a lot of things. Things that are too complicated to explain."

Lowering his head, Quintin pressed his mouth to her ear. "Try me, Vicky. I'm a good listener."

Victoria surprised Quintin when she clung to him, burying her face against his T-shirt. "I can't, Quintin. I can't tell you now."

His arms tightened around her waist. "I'll wait, Vicky.

I'll wait until you feel comfortable enough to tell me. And whatever it is, it can't be so bad . . ."

She put her fingers over his mouth, stopping his words. "No more," she ordered quietly.

Quintin captured her fingers and kissed each one before running his tongue over her soft palm, eliciting the trembling response he sought from her.

Pulling her hand free, she gasped, "Quintin, don't. You act as if there's only the two of us on this boat."

Removing his sunglasses, he stared at her. "If that were the case, then I would be faced with a dilemma. Do I drop anchor and make love to you on deck or try to go below where I'd take you in one of the cabins. Yes, Vicky, I want you."

She wasn't given the opportunity to reply because he walked away, leaving her staring at his broad back.

Swaying slightly, she leaned against the railing and tried valiantly to bring her emotions under control.

He knew. Without a doubt he knew that she wanted him to make love to her.

It didn't matter that he was in love with another woman. It didn't matter that she would never marry Quintin or give him children. All that mattered was that they wanted each other. Sharing her body with Quintin was inevitable. The only question that remained was where or when.

Jo escorted Ryan across the deck. The boy's tightly closed eyes and swaying gait indicated the ship's rolling motion was upsetting him.

Ryan's knees buckled, and Ethan rushed to him, lifting him effortlessly into his arms. Sandy's eyebrows furrowed in concern. "Are you all right, son?"

Ryan nodded. "My stomach keeps moving, Ethan."

"Take him below and I'll fix him something that'll settle his stomach," Jo volunteered.

"Stomachaches are for girls," Ryan mumbled, turning his face toward Ethan's broad chest.

Ethan chuckled, his hazel eyes sweeping from Jo to Victoria. "Stomachaches aren't just for girls. Men get them, too."

Victoria watched Ethan, Ryan, and Jo disappear below the deck of the ship, shaking her head. Males, she thought. The moment they left the womb they became sexist.

She remained on deck, inhaling the saltwater and enjoying the feel of the sun until it became too hot.

Climbing down into the hatch, she was surrounded by smooth and gleaming wood walls and doors. The door to one cabin stood open and she saw Ethan sitting on a bunk while Jo sat on another beside Ryan, coaxing the child to drink the liquid in the cup she held to his mouth.

Moving closer to the bow, she discovered a large galley, modern and fully equipped for a life at sea. Victoria had sailed before on sloops, catamarans, and tenders. She was more than aware of the cost for these vessels. It appeared as if Quintin Lord had spared no expense for what he called his *"addiction." Jamila* was an exquisite sailing ship.

She unpacked the large chest, storing perishables in an ample refrigerator. She emptied Jo's large bag and extracted cooking utensils and china.

Thirty minutes later, the hold of the ship was filled with the aroma of frying bacon and simmering coffee. Freshly baked croissants were wrapped in a clean towel and left warming in a small oven.

It took several seconds, but Victoria registered silence and stillness. The engines had stopped.

She heard the sound of someone clearing his throat, and she turned to find Quintin and Ethan crowding the doorway to the galley.

"Breakfast smells good," Quintin quipped with a wide grin. Ethan nodded in agreement.

Jo pushed the two men aside and washed her hands in

a stainless-steel sink. Taking a half-dozen eggs from a carton, she cracked them in a large aluminum bowl.

"What time do we eat?" Quintin questioned.

Victoria glanced over at Jo, who nodded perceptively. "You don't," they chorused in unison.

"We . . . we don't," Ethan replied, his voice nearly breaking in disappointment.

Victoria folded her hands on her hips. "You 'men' didn't want the 'ladies' to bring anything. I remember Captain Lord saying that men only bring what's on their backs when they go sailing, not vanity mirrors."

Ethan's attractive dimpled chin dropped as his gaze swung to his friend's face. "No, man, you didn't say that, did you?"

"Answer your first mate, Captain Lord," Victoria taunted.

Ethan crossed his arms over his chest, glaring at Quintin as Jo beat the egg mixture with a wire whisk.

Victoria's hands were busy sectioning oranges into halves, a sly smile lifting the corners of her mouth. *Beg, Quintin,* she ordered silently.

Ethan stepped into the galley, his tall frame making the space appear smaller. "Apologize, Quintin," he threatened, his gaze fixed on the strips of bacon on a large platter. The aroma of brown sugar and cinnamon rose from the crisp, golden-browned meat.

"Quin-tin," Victoria drawled.

"No!" His reply was adamant.

Ethan panicked. "Hell, I'll apologize." Bowing slightly from the waist, he bobbed to Victoria and Jo. "I'm sorry, ladies, if I offended you."

Reaching over, Jo picked up a stack of plates and handed them to Ethan. "Please take these up on deck."

Ethan, ignoring Quintin's scowl, took the plates and pushed past him. Jo picked up a tablecloth, a stack of cloth napkins, and a handful of cutlery and followed Ethan.

Quintin stalked into the galley and trapped Victoria against a wall. "You're a wicked woman, Victoria Jones."

She stared at the middle of his chest, biting back laughter. "Beg, Quintin," she crooned.

Bracing a hand on either side of her head, he leaned forward. Lowering his head, his mouth grazed her cheek. "You don't know how much I want you, Vicky. Please let me make love to you."

She pounded his shoulders with her fists. "Not that kind of begging, Quintin."

He caught her small fists, grinning. "That's the only kind of begging I know." He noted the set of her stubborn little chin. "Okay, Victoria Jones. I apologize for my off-color, sexist remark. Now can I eat?"

Rising on tiptoe, she kissed his mouth, running her tongue over his lower lip. "Aye, aye, sir."

Quintin watched as Victoria cooked the eggs to a soft yellow fluffiness and turned them over into a dish that would keep them warm. He helped carry a jug of freshly squeezed orange juice in cracked ice and the basket of croissants up on deck.

Ethan had helped Jo set the table with a white-and-blue checkered tablecloth and cobalt-blue napkins. The blue-and-white color scheme was repeated in the bone-white china plates with shimmering cobalt-blue trim. The wind had settled down to less than three knots, and when the four adults sat down at the table, Quintin had to admit to himself that the presence of the two women added a touch of class that *Jamila* had not experienced in the past.

Ethan lay on a deck chair, his bare feet crossed at the ankles. Closing his eyes, he smiled. "Did you beg good, buddy?"

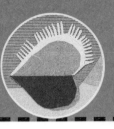

Quintin didn't stir from his lounging position. "Think I didn't? Etta Mae Lord didn't raise no fool."

"Is Victoria the one?"

Quintin, his gaze fixed on Victoria as she sat on the deck playing cards with Jo and Ryan, smiled. "Yes."

Crossing his arms over his chest and settling into a more comfortable position, Ethan grinned. "Good choice, buddy."

Thirteen

Jamila prowled the waters of the Chesapeake for hours until Quintin dropped anchor at Cape Charles. Everyone was ready for a light lunch.

Victoria lifted a curling french fry from Quintin's plate. "I can't believe I'm still hungry," she confessed.

"Sailing always gives me a tremendous appetite," Ethan said, reaching for the hamburger on Ryan's plate.

"Hey!" Ryan cried out. "I wanted that."

Ethan took a large bite out of the burger. "I'll buy you another," he replied after swallowing. "Better yet, what do you say we pick up a half dozen lobsters and go back to my place and have cocktails and lobster under the stars?"

"Sounds good to me," Quintin replied, his gaze fixed on Victoria's face.

Ethan smiled at Jo. "Will you join us?" She stared at him through the lenses of her sunglasses.

"I'd love to," she agreed.

"I'll have the lobster, but I'll pass on the cocktails," Ryan quipped.

Everyone laughed at Ryan's serious expression. Ethan dropped an arm around his son's shoulders and hugged him. Ryan returned the affectionate gesture while at the same time retrieving what was left of his burger from Ethan's plate.

He stared at the half-eaten grilled beef patty. "I think you're better than Popeye's Wimpy, Ethan."

"I'll Wimpy you," Ethan growled, holding Ryan's head in a loose headlock and rubbing the knuckles of his right hand over the boy's hair.

Victoria smiled at the good-natured teasing between Ethan and Ryan, but she thought it odd that the boy insisted on calling his father by his given name. She glanced over at Quintin and he returned her stare, winking.

"We can sail into Norfolk and pick up the lobsters, then head home," Quintin stated.

Ethan winced. "I don't think Hannibal will appreciate a half dozen live lobsters on board. Remember when he attacked the bushel of the crabs?"

Quintin groaned. "Don't remind me," he said, relating how he and Ethan had gone out on *Jamila* for her maiden voyage and picked up a bushel of crabs at a wharf along the Virginia coast for a fish-fry later that evening.

"The basket was covered, but Hannibal was transfixed by all of the thrashing and scratching, so he decided to investigate. He tipped the bushel over, and crabs were everywhere. Most of them had made their way successfully back to the ocean before I could drop anchor and help Ethan retrieve them."

Victoria, Ryan, and Jo laughed until they were breathless as Ethan described in great detail the sound of their claws clicking like castanets on *Jamila*'s highly polished deck.

"Quintin went absolutely ballistic because they were ruining his deck. But what I couldn't understand was that he was picking up the little buggers and pitching them back in the basket while screaming, 'Throw the scavengers overboard, Ethan.' Meanwhile, Hannibal was running around barking like he was possessed, his toenails leaving long jagged scratches every time he came to an abrupt stop whenever a crab turned in his direction."

Quintin nodded. "*Jamila*'s maiden voyage was quite a catastrophe. We managed to salvage about two dozen crabs, and I had to have the deck refinished before I could take her out again."

Jo, wiping her damp eyes, said, "I guess lobster is out."

"Not if it's lobster tails," Victoria replied.

Ethan's smile was dazzling. "Good call, Victoria. How many can you eat, buddy?" he asked Quintin.

"Three if they're small."

"Ryan?"

Ryan puffed up his narrow chest, his brow furrowed in concentration. "Four if they're small."

Ethan gave him a skeptical look. "Victoria?"

"Two."

Ethan turned to Jo, his expression impassive. "How about you, Jo?"

Jo's expression was equally closed. "Two."

Victoria glanced from her friend to Ethan, wondering why the redhead was so subdued with Quintin's friend. Had Ethan said something to her that turned her off?

"Twenty tails should be enough, wouldn't you say, Quintin?"

"Ask Victoria. She's the master chef."

Ethan leaned back on his chair, realization widening his gaze. "No wonder breakfast was so incredible. Victoria Jones, you can cook for me anytime."

Quintin's jaw clenched. "No, she can't," he countered softly.

"Why not?" Ethan had missed Quintin's challenge.

"Because she cooks for *me*."

Ethan's body stiffened. At thirty-eight, he was more than experienced enough to recognize territorial possession, and he had just stepped over the boundary.

Victoria felt her face heat up as Quintin, Ethan, and Jo stared at her. Ryan was still too young to understand the sexual undercurrent surrounding the adults at the table.

Ethan's gaze returned to Quintin and he nodded, acknowledging the other man's claim. He turned to Victoria, flashing his charming smile. "Do you cater events?"

"I do." She managed to give Ethan a polite smile. "If you have something in mind I'll give you my number and we'll talk at another time."

The heat had left her face, but she still felt rage coursing through her chest. Quintin did not own her. He had no right to assume she would cook only for him. After all, cooking was her profession and livelihood. The look she shot Quintin said, "We'll talk later."

Quintin rose to his feet, aware that he had angered Victoria. He knew her well enough to note the narrowing of her eyes and the set of her mouth.

He hadn't meant for his statement to come out the way it had, but he hadn't been able to help himself. He had allowed jealousy to cloud his judgment even though he knew Ethan would never attempt to come on to Victoria.

He would apologize to her, or if necessary he would beg. He was becoming quite proficient in the begging department.

Coming around to her side of the table, he helped her to her feet. Leaning over, he sang softly in her ear, "Ain't Too Proud To Beg."

"Quintin, behave," she gasped, taking a sharp breath and glancing around to see if the others had overheard him.

"I am," he whispered back, grasping her hand and leading her down the pier toward *Jamila.*

Forgetting about her earlier anger, she smiled up at him. "You just won't do right."

Without warning, he bent down and swung her up in his arms singing loudly, "Do Right Woman, Do Right Man."

Burying her face between his strong neck and solid shoulder, Victoria laughed until the tears flowed down her cheeks.

Quintin's theatrics set the mood for the return trip. The four adults launched a repertoire of Golden Oldies to show tunes while Ryan lounged on deck beside Hannibal, shaking his head in amazement.

He pressed his face to Hannibal's ear, whispering, "It's enough to make me seasick again. Grown-ups are whacko."

The informal gathering began in earnest with Jo arranging a bouquet of white roses and irises from Ethan's garden for the large table set up in the rear of the cottage. She also cut several bunches of scented herbs, adding a delicate fragrance to the humid night air.

Quintin placed tall beeswax candles in a half dozen antique Spanish lanterns and hung them from nearby trees. He also filled amber-colored votive glasses with white votive lights. Lighting them, he placed the flickering lights strategically at one end of the table.

Victoria and Ethan had claimed the cooking duties, broiling the lobster tails, preparing a dipping sauce and a salad of torn red leaf lettuce, dandelion leaves, and roasted red peppers in a balsamic vinegar dressing. She also quickly and expertly turned two overly ripe avocados into a spicy guacamole. Jo helped, slicing sourdough bread and brushing each slice with garlic butter, then warming it in the oven.

Later there was only the sound of a classical guitar composition coming through the speakers set up outdoors as the diners concentrated on devouring everything put out on the table.

The setting sun and the flickering of fireflies and the candles created a mood that was quiet and almost ethereal. Ethan had served an excellent vintage white wine, and after two glasses Victoria reclined on the grass beside Ryan and stared up at the lanterns.

"You cook better than Ethan," Ryan stated, matter-of-factly. "And he's a good cook."

"I'm only good because I've been trained to cook."

Turning his head slightly, Ryan stared at her profile. "Maybe you and Ethan can get married, then both of you can cook together."

Victoria turned her head slowly and stared at the tortured expression on the young boy's face. "Your father isn't married?"

Ryan bit down on his lower lip. "Ethan is not my father. Well, not yet anyway. He wants to adopt me, then he'll be my father and I'll be his son. It's going to take a long time. I told him it would go faster if he had a wife, but he says he doesn't need a wife to adopt me."

Victoria swallowed painfully. Now she knew why the child referred to Ethan as "Ethan."

"He's right, Ryan. Nowadays a person doesn't have to be married to adopt a child."

"But it would go faster if he was married. I like being with Ethan. I hate going back to that . . ."

Victoria sat up and stared down at Ryan. His eyes were tightly closed, as if he willed tears not to fall. "Back to what, Ryan?"

"Back to that place." He bit down on his lower lip. "People steal my things!"

Without thinking, Victoria pulled the child from the grass and held him gently. "Don't give up, Ryan. Ethan wants you as much as you want him."

The boy's large, dark eyes were trusting. "Are you sure?"

She nodded slowly. "Very sure. I don't know Ethan very well, but I can see that he loves you.

"I love him, too."

Victoria was surprised that a child his age could express his feelings so openly to a stranger. Hugging him, she kissed his forehead. "How about dessert?"

Ryan groaned and pulled out of her loose embrace. "I can't. I ate two lobster tails."

Victoria had only been able to eat one. Ethan had purchased twenty lobster tails, each weighing close to one pound. The meat from the uneaten tails could easily be used for a salad or a bisque.

Quintin sat with his back propped against a large oak tree, watching Victoria and Ryan. An indescribable feeling had tightened his chest when he saw her fold the boy in her arms. The gesture was so tender, so touching, that it stunned him, and at that moment he thought of her suckling his child at her breasts.

And if he thought what he felt for her was just infatuation it was easily dismissed. He *did* love her. He loved her with an emotion that went so deep, he would not have been able to put it into words.

He tore his gaze away from her and smiled. Ethan and Jo sat at the table talking quietly. Victoria's friend was quiet and shy. Almost as shy as Quintin before you got to know him well.

Hannibal ambled over to Quintin and lay down beside him, muzzle on his master's thigh. Quintin scratched his pet behind the ears, closing his eyes. The day had been successful. He had taken *Jamila* out to sea with Victoria; at one time he would have been content to sail with Hannibal, but now sailing would not be the same unless Victoria was aboard.

A satisfied smile curled his lips under the mustache as his thoughts were filled with a tiny woman with clear red-brown skin, liquid eyes, and a full mouth.

At that moment Quintin made himself a promise. He would marry Victoria Jones before the New Year.

Fourteen

As the votive lights burned out, the flickering candles in the lanterns provided the only source of illumination in the encroaching darkness, competing with the stars in a navy-blue sky.

Ryan had fallen asleep, his head resting against Victoria's shoulder. She shifted to a more comfortable position and cradled the boy to her breasts, smiling.

The day had been wonderful. She had fallen in love with *Jamila.* The ship was exquisitely designed to provide the utmost comfort.

Her smile broadened. Quintin had proven to be an excellent captain and host, and she knew that she loved him with all of her heart. Her smiled faded slowly as she tried comparing her feelings for Quintin with how she had felt about Richard.

Richard Morgan had always been unreachable, unattainable. Maybe that was why she'd had a crush on him. Richard was older than her by eight years and that alone was attraction enough. He was an "older" man.

He was older *and* controlling. The selection and the decorating of their home was the only area where she had had absolute authority. Richard Morgan did not trouble himself with something he considered "a woman's domain."

He abhorred her dance career, tolerating it only because he knew if he wanted Victoria Jones, he had to accept her profession. He felt dancers—even ballet dancers—were a degenerate lot without a shred of morality.

Victoria wanted to dance from the first time she saw Tchaikovsky's *Nutcracker.* She began dancing lessons at eight, and became a professional at twelve when she earned the coveted role as Clara in an all-black adaptation of the popular Christmas ballet.

If only Richard had waited he would have had his wish. She was forced to give up her dance career, but what Victoria hadn't known until that time was that he wanted an heir more than he resented her dancing.

Sighing, Victoria dropped a kiss on the top of Ryan's head. She held a child who was crying out for a mother and father, and she wanted a child. Even if she couldn't bear a child she was more than willing to adopt one. A child who would be more special than one who was of her own flesh because she would be given the option of choosing. If she had had a child with Richard she would have accepted and loved it unconditionally. But with adoption she could select the sex, age, racial designation, or ethnicity of her son or daughter.

Ethan and Ryan were blessed. They wanted each other enough to wait; wait forever if necessary.

"Is he heavy?"

She started, staring up at Quintin who hunkered down beside her. "No." Her voice was low and breathless.

Quintin smiled, noting the startled look in her eyes. The candles in the three overhead lanterns' sputtered, casting a soft glow across her features.

"Are you ready to go home?"

"Yes," Victoria replied, returning his smile. She hadn't realized she was tired until she sat down. She had been up before dawn rolling dough for the croissants.

Quintin eased Ryan from Victoria's embrace, lifting the boy. He walked over to Ethan, depositing him in his foster father's outstretched arms.

"We're going to push off now," he informed Ethan.

Ethan nodded, smiling. "Thanks for everything, buddy."

"My thanks to you, too, for the lobster. We must do it again."

Ethan arched an eyebrow. "Only if it's the same crew."

"Same crew," Quintin confirmed, smiling at Jo.

She lowered her head, blushing furiously in the waning light. "Thank you, Ethan."

"The pleasure has been all mine," he returned, his gaze fixed on her lowered head. His attention was diverted as Victoria moved over to stand beside Quintin. "I hope I'll get to see you again, Victoria."

She gave him an open smile. "But of course." Her gaze swept over Ryan. "You have a wonderful son, Ethan."

Ethan tightened his grip, pulling Ryan closer to his chest. "Thank you. He's the most precious thing in my life."

"It's been great, Ethan," Jo said, her mysterious smile hinting of something left unsaid.

Ethan nodded. "Same here."

Quintin led Victoria, Jo, and Hannibal back to his four-wheeler. There was complete silence on the return trip. Everyone was exhausted from a day filled with sun, salt-water, and rich food.

Jo refused Victoria's offer to spend the night, claiming she had to be back in Washington to coordinate a wedding breakfast.

She hugged Victoria while Quintin put her overnight bag in the trunk of her car. "I'll call you tomorrow night," she whispered conspiratorially. Turning to Quintin, she rose on tiptoe and kissed his cheek. "Thanks for every-thing, Quintin."

Quintin gathered her to his chest and kissed her fore-head. "Does this mean you're willing to sail with the ty-rannical Captain Lord again?"

"Aye, aye, sir."

He released Jo, chuckling under his breath. Victoria's friend was all right.

They waited until Jo drove off, then walked up the stairs to their respective apartments. Victoria opened her door and Quintin carried the chest into the kitchen, placing it on a counter.

"Are you up to walking tomorrow morning, Vicky?"

She offered a tired smile. "Of course."

Quintin pulled her to his chest, kissing her cheek. "Sleep well."

She stared at his back as he walked out of the kitchen. Minutes later, she turned out the lights and made her way up the curving staircase to her own bedroom. She checked the messages on her answering machine, bathed, fell into her bed and was asleep within minutes.

Victoria lay awake, listening to the sound of rain pelting the windows. She had slept fitfully. She had been bone tired but dreams about Richard and Quintin attacked her relentlessly throughout the night.

Pressing her face into a pillow, she groaned. Sleep was elusive, so she decided to get up.

Not bothering to go through her stretching routine at the barre, she headed for the bathroom and stood under the cool spray of the shower until her flesh was beaded with an icy exhilaration. There was something to be said for a cold shower.

She toweled herself dry and creamed her body. The doorbell chimed melodiously as she pulled a slip dress over her head. Glancing at the clock on the bedside table, she winced. It was seven o'clock. Quintin was insane if he thought she was going to walk in the rain. Skipping lightly down the stairs in her bare feet, she opened the door.

"Good morning, beautiful."

Victoria returned Quintin's sensual smile, her gaze sweeping over his tall frame in a single glance. This morning he wore a pair of jeans, bleached a near white from numerous washings, and a white tank top that displayed his well-toned upper body to perfection. His feet were bare.

"Get back into bed, Vicky," he ordered, holding up two large white shopping bags.

"What are you doing?"

"Don't make me beg, Vicky,"

She crossed her arms under her breasts, grinning. "Beg, Quintin," she crooned. "I love it when you beg."

He headed toward her and she backpedaled to the staircase, deciding to play along with him. "Aren't you going to tell me why you want me in bed?"

"I'll show you," Quintin replied, turning suddenly and walking into her kitchen.

Victoria retreated up the staircase to her bedroom. She straightened the sheet on the bed, turned back the blanket and fluffed up the pillows. She slipped into bed seconds before Quintin strode into the room carrying a tray, setting it down across her lap.

"There's nothing more romantic than sharing breakfast in bed on a rainy day." Leaning over, he dropped a kiss on the top of her head. "You can start without me."

Victoria uncovered a Styrofoam container. It was filled with a stack of buckwheat pancakes. The tray also held packets of butter, coffee creamer, maple syrup, plastic utensils wrapped in a paper napkin, and a Styrofoam cup of steaming black coffee.

Quintin returned, carrying his own tray. He balanced it while getting into bed beside Victoria. "Why don't you select something nice to listen to while we eat," he suggested, motioning with his head at the radio on the table on her side of the bed.

Victoria lowered her chin and peered up at him from

under her lashes. "My, my, my. Aren't we bossy this morning."

He settled back against the pillows. "I brave the elements for my neighbor to bring her breakfast and what does she do? Nag, nag, nag."

"What your neighbor is going to do is kiss you passionately after she finishes her breakfast," she promised.

Quintin's lips curved up in a smile. "You break your promises, Victoria. There was another time when you promised to kiss my cheek and make it all better."

She gave him a sidelong glance. "I'll keep it this morning."

His hands stilled and he stared at her profile. "This is *one* morning that I'll make certain you keep it."

Victoria tried concentrating on her breakfast as the heat from Quintin's body seeped into hers.

She couldn't believe she was sitting in bed with Quintin casually eating a stack of fluffy pancakes from a take-out restaurant as if it something they did every morning.

"Nice music," he mumbled after taking a swallow of coffee. Victoria had selected a station that played soft, easy-listening music. The melodious strains of a musical rendition of "Midnight Train To Georgia" floated from the speakers.

"Wonderful pancakes," she complimented. The buckwheat cakes were light and flavorful.

"The cook down at Ray's Diner is exceptional," Quintin explained. "When I walked in this morning everyone asked if I'd been away."

"Did you tell them that you now have your own private chef?"

Leaning over, Quintin kissed her ear. "No. That's our secret."

Victoria glanced up, registering the merriment in his gaze. "What other secrets are you hiding?"

"I have a cleaning woman."

She nearly spilled the coffee in her container when she brought it up to her mouth. "You *what?*"

He flashed a pained expression. "You wounded me deeply when you called my place a hovel. I happen to know what hovel means, Victoria."

She felt her face burn with embarrassment. "I didn't mean . . ."

"Yes you did mean it," he countered. "And you were right. And you're not the first woman who has commented on how I keep my house."

Victoria wondered if that woman was the one he was in love with. Was she also turned off by the piles of clothes and clutter strewn throughout the spacious apartment.

"My mother has refused to come to visit because she's ashamed by how I live. Her house is always spotless and she can't understand how I can live with clothes on the floor and trash piled up for days."

"The woman is your mother?" Victoria couldn't help smiling.

Quintin nodded. "The one and only Etta Mae."

She laughed. "I think I like Etta Mae."

"How would you like to meet her?"

"When?"

"Tomorrow. We usually all get together for a Memorial Day cookout. Etta Mae has been after me for years to bring a 'nice girl' with me."

Victoria felt her pulse quicken. Why hadn't Quintin asked his leggy girlfriend to go with him to his family's holiday gathering?

"I'll pass this time," she said.

"Are you busy tomorrow?"

"No," she answered honestly.

"Then why not come with me?"

Because a man usually doesn't bring a woman to meet his family, especially his mother, unless he's serious about her, she thought.

"I don't want to intrude," she said instead. "It's going to be a family gathering."

Quintin stared down at her hands, noting the slight trembling. He placed his larger hand over hers, squeezing gently. "If your parents asked you to bring someone to a family celebration and you asked me, I'd go and not once would I feel like an intruder, Vicky. I'd be your guest."

How could she tell him that she was willing to sleep with him, but nothing more than that. That their relationship would be similar to the one she had had with Masud in Paris.

Girding herself with resolve, she nodded. "Okay, Quintin. I'm ready to meet Etta Mae."

"She'll adore you," he stated, squeezing her fingers before releasing them.

Both of them finished their breakfast in silence, the sound of music competing with the rhythmic beating of the falling rain.

Quintin took both trays, swinging his legs out of the bed. "Don't go away," he ordered softly.

Victoria couldn't go anywhere if she tried. She was too full. Hanging out with Quintin Lord was going to make her fat.

Sliding down under the blanket, she closed her eyes and smiled. He had become so much a part of her life in the short time since she had moved into the apartment that she found it difficult to remember when he hadn't been there. In only three weeks he had become so inexorably involved in her life that she didn't know where it began or ended.

There were times when he disappeared for days, but she still felt an invisible, tenuous thread weaving them together. She hadn't wanted to fall in love with Quintin Lord, but she had. However, she was realistic enough to know that she could not plan a future with him. She would take what he offered and give him what she could in return, and when it was over it would be over.

Quintin reentered the bedroom and turned off the bedside lamp. The gray sky and falling rain darkened the room, not permitting light through the Palladian windows.

He slipped into the bed beside Victoria, pulling her gently into his arms. Her heat and fragrance washed over him as he inhaled deeply.

Victoria nuzzled her nose to his warm throat. "Thank you for a wonderful breakfast," she breathed out softly.

"You're quite welcome." His voice was low and soothing.

"You were right," she said after a long, comfortable silence.

"About what?"

"Having breakfast in bed on a rainy day is very romantic."

"Hmmm," he groaned, settling her against his body and pulling her left leg over his jean-covered thighs.

Victoria wiggled until she found a comfortable position against the hard male body. His arms tightened around her back and minutes later she fell into a deep, dreamless sleep.

Quintin rested his chin on the top of Victoria's head, luxuriating in the press of her tiny body against his. Nestled in his arms, asleep, she was so soft and trusting. He held her, her head resting on his shoulder until he, too, fell asleep.

The sound of their breathing, the music coming from the radio, and the incessant tapping of rain against the windows swallowed them whole in a cocoon of love and peace.

Fifteen

A rumble of thunder shook Victoria, and she came awake with a violent start.

"It's all right, darling. It's only the storm."

She blinked in the darkness, trying to reorient herself. Relaxing, she snuggled closer to Quintin. "How long have I been asleep?"

His fingers trailed over her back. *"We've* been asleep for over an hour," he said softly near her ear.

"You're not good for me, Quintin.

He chuckled. "Why not?"

"Eating in bed, then falling asleep. I'm going to get fat," she complained.

"You'll never be fat," he retorted, pulling back and trying to see her features in the darkened room. "Maybe you'll gain some weight in the hips, but never fat." His hands cradled the fullness of her buttocks. "I wouldn't mind if you added a few inches to your caboose."

Her face heated up. "Quintin!"

He laughed openly. "Some men like legs, others big breasts. I prefer cabooses." His right hand searched under the hem of the skimpy cotton slip dress, grazing the backs of her thighs. It continued its slow, deliberate journey, ending with his fingers splayed over the triangle of satin hiding her femininity.

Quintin's gentle touch sent currents of desire racing through Victoria. His hand continued its exploration, sweeping over her belly and breasts. Her entire body was on fire, flushed with pinpoints of simmering heat.

"Quintin," she moaned. Whatever else she wanted to say was left unsaid as his hand came up, his thumb going to her chin. Exerting the slightest pressure, he opened her mouth.

His tongue traced the outline of her mouth with an agonizing slowness before it slipped through her parted lips. His tongue worked its magic, moving in and out of her mouth and precipitating a familiar throbbing between her thighs.

She had become a lump of soft clay with Quintin Lord the sculptor. He could mold her into whatever shape and form he desired.

Victoria couldn't get close enough to him as she pressed her full, aching breasts to his chest. It was as if her clothes burned her sensitive flesh. She was on fire—everywhere.

Her hands searched under the cotton fabric of his tank top, fingertips feathering over the solid muscles in his broad chest and leaving tracks in the thick mat of chest hair. The hair on his body excited her. Richard's skin had been almost as smooth as her own.

"Vicky. Oh, Vicky," Quintin chanted hoarsely, his hands roaming intimately over her breasts. Withdrawing his hand, his mouth replaced his fingers.

Gasping aloud, she arched. Her nipples exploded in a pebble hardness against the ridge of his teeth. Writhing beneath him, Victoria couldn't stop the moans from escaping her parted lips.

Quintin, his mouth fastened to one breast then the other, murmured a silent prayer he could prolong the foreplay. His body was on the verge of exploding.

He had fantasized about Victoria Jones from the first moment he saw her, and knowing that fantasy was to be fulfilled was an awesome thought to him.

The storm raging outside matched the rising passion of the two lovers as their private world was rocked with one discovery after another.

Quintin undressed Victoria, quickly removing the slip dress and her bikini panties, while she struggled to pull his tank top over his wide shoulders. Brushing her hands away, he rose to his knees and divested himself of his shirt, jeans, and briefs. Pushing the mound of clothes to the floor, he reached for her.

The thunder rumbled and shook the heavens while the sky and the bedroom were lit up by the flash of lightning, but it did not match the searing passion of Victoria and Quintin.

Quintin moved over her, his hands beneath her hips. She felt his hard pulsing length against her belly, and her breasts tingled against his hair-roughened chest.

She caressed the length of his back, aware of the unleashed power in his strong male body.

He trailed a series of slow, shivery kisses down her neck, whispering her name. She breathed lightly between parted lips, crooning, "Quintin. Oh, oh!"

He answered her, taking her right hand and pressing it to his groin. Her fingers circled him, squeezing gently.

The breath rushed from Quintin. His body was rigid with poised ecstasy. His hand covered hers and he guided his throbbing sex into her wetness.

She moaned softly and he cradled her face between his palms, kissing her mouth. "I'm sorry, baby. I had no idea you were that small and tight."

Victoria, eyes closed, felt every inch of Quintin as her flesh sheathed his. The enormity of their act washed over her. What was she doing? He didn't love her. He was in love with another woman.

Quintin sensed the change in Victoria. He could not continue. He didn't want to make love to her. He wanted her to make love *with* him; make love to each other.

Supporting his greater weight on his elbows, he pressed his lips to her ear. "What's the matter, darling?"

Victoria's arms went around his strong neck. She wanted to cry; cry because she loved him so much. She buried her face in his throat, breathing heavily.

"Do you not want me to make love to you?" he asked when she didn't respond.

She shook her head.

Quintin doubted whether he would have been able to withdraw from her body; even though he hadn't moved he was close to erupting within her.

His eyes opened and he groaned audibly as realization swept over him in a cold wave. It was the first time—the very first time—that he hadn't protected the woman during a sexual encounter.

"Vicky . . . Vicky," he repeated, his heart pounding loudly in his ears. He was certain she could hear it. "I'm sorry. I should've protected you."

"I won't get pregnant," she stated, allaying his fear.

Quintin took that to mean she was utilizing a form of contraception. Exhaling, he smiled. "And I can assure you that I'm not carrying any sexually transmitted disease."

"Thank you, Quintin." Her tone was expressionless.

His passion dissipated like someone letting the air out of a balloon. He couldn't make love to her—not now. Withdrawing, he reversed their positions. She lay on his chest, flesh against flesh.

"Do you want to talk about it, Vicky?"

"No." Her voice was soft and void of emotion. What she wanted to say was that she loved him; she loved him enough to want to spend the rest of her life with him, that she wanted to become his wife, that she would be willing to become the mother of all of the children they wanted to adopt. But that was not going to happen because he was in love with another woman; another woman would become his wife and the mother of his biological children.

Reaching down, Quintin pulled the sheet up over their bodies. He held her tightly in the darkened bedroom until they fell asleep for the second time that morning.

Victoria awoke, her body covered with moisture. The heat from Quintin's body was overpowering.

She couldn't believe she had fallen asleep on top of him; her legs nestled within his.

"Where are you going?" he asked as she tried slipping out of his arms.

Her nose grazed his mustache as he lowered his head to stare down at her. "I need a shower." He released her and she slid off the bed.

Walking into the bathroom, she opened the door to the shower stall and turned on the water, adjusting the temperature and the flow of water.

Stepping into the stall, she closed the door and raised her face. The warm water sluiced down her hair, flattening it to her scalp. She rinsed away the scent of Quintin's body, then reached for a bar of fragrant hard-milled soap.

She soaped her body, shampooed her hair, but before she could add her customary instant conditioner the shower door opened and Quintin joined her.

The soft overhead light permitted Victoria to see what the darkened bedroom had not revealed. The breath was sucked out of her lungs as her gaze swept over Quintin's naked body. He was Michelangelo's David come to life.

He gave her a shy smile. "I thought you'd need someone to do your back."

Her large eyes crinkled in laughter as she turned around. Quintin moved closer, pressing his chest to her back, his arms circling her waist.

"I'm going to do your back," he crooned softly against

her ear, "and your neck and your breasts." He punctuated his promise, his fingers splaying over her soap-covered breasts.

His fingers began their own magic, sweeping slowly over the small firm globes of flesh until her nipples hardened. He turned her around and panting, her chest heaving, she pressed her cheek to his shoulder.

Quintin's lids lowered over his gold-brown eyes as he felt his passion for Victoria spiral again. He had lain in bed, cursing himself for not making love to her. She hadn't said he couldn't make love to her, and the image of her naked and writhing beneath him propelled him from her bed.

He wanted Victoria Jones. But more than that, he loved Victoria Jones!

Brushing back the strands of wet hair clinging to her forehead, he smiled down at her. "I love you," he whispered reverently.

Victoria would have fallen if he hadn't been holding her. Her lower lip trembled as she melted against his strong body. "Quintin!" she breathed out, not believing what she had heard.

Her arms went around his neck and she arched her feet until she was standing on her toes. Her mouth closed on his as her love flowed from her to communicate silently that she also loved him.

Quintin was overwhelmed by her response. His hands encircled her waist and he picked her up. Holding her with one arm, he used one hand and guided his member into her tight, warm pulsing body as water flowed over them. Her hot flesh closed around him and he groaned audibly.

Victoria tightened her legs around his waist, leaning back in his strong grip. Knowing Quintin loved her increased her desire and she responded to him, giving him everything, holding nothing back.

Her body felt hot, then cold and then more heat. She breathed in deep soul-shattering drafts of air as Quintin quickened his thrusts, their bodies finding a tempo that reached a shattering crescendo.

Quintin's back, pressed against a tiled wall, made a downward journey. He took Victoria with him. He couldn't believe the passion shaking his legs and not permitting him to stand. He sat on the floor of the shower stall, his body joined with hers. The cooling water temperature did not cool his desire. Long, strong fingers encircled her tiny waist, and he guided her up and down over his blood-engorged sex.

He kissed her deeply, his tongue keeping the same rhythm as his thrusting body. He heard her gasps of pleasure, and his own gasps and moans joined Victoria's.

He had known the moment he saw her that she was different—she was the one.

Victoria moaned aloud with erotic pleasure, Quintin's hardness electrifying her. She rose and fell to meet him in an uncontrolled passion, and then it happened. Waves of ecstasy swept over her as she ground her buttocks against his thighs. Heat rippled through her. There was no way she could disguise her body's reaction to his lovemaking.

Quintin's passion rose to meet and overlap hers when he exploded inside her body. The heat clouded his brain, singed his body, and he surrendered all that he had as liquid passion poured from him and bathed her with love.

They sat on the tiled floor, breathing heavily while the falling water cooled. Victoria laid her forehead against Quintin's chest, trying to catch her breath.

She couldn't believe her response to him. She had never responded to a man with such abandon. Smiling, she savored the feeling of complete satisfaction.

Quintin's breathing slowed. He experienced twin emotions of shock and contentment. He had never taken a woman the way he had just made love to Victoria, but never had he experienced the feeling of sweet satisfaction that made him almost as helpless as a newborn.

He didn't know where he found the strength, but he gathered Victoria from the floor of the shower stall and rinsed her hair and body. The water was icy cold when they finally stepped out of the stall.

They laughed like small children, drying each other's body with thick fluffy towels. Victoria admired the beauty of his male form as she drew the terry-cloth fabric down his spine.

She kissed his shoulders. "You have a very nice butt, Mr. Lord," she crooned, her fingers gripping his firm hips.

Quintin nearly choked. He spun around, taking the towel from her loose grip. "You're wicked, Vicky."

Arching her eyebrows, she smiled up at him. "I don't think so, Quintin. I don't believe I have a wicked bone in my body."

Moving closer to her, he pulled her head to his chest. "And what a fabulous little body you have."

She rubbed her nose against his chest hair. "You've just confirmed something you told me the night you promised to show me your watercolors."

"What's that?"

"You *are* good, Quintin. Very, very good."

They made their way back to the bedroom and the bed. Both of them were content to lie beside the other, holding hands, lost in their own private thoughts.

They made love for the second time, this joining a slow and tender one. They slept again, sated, and when they awoke their passions had been slaked—until the next time.

It was early evening and the rain had slacked to a soft-falling mist. Victoria sat beside Quintin on the patio enjoying the warm damp night. The candles flickering in the living room cast a golden glow through the screen of the sliding patio doors.

Quintin tightened his grip on Victoria's shoulders and kissed her hair. She had allowed it to air dry. Spending the whole day with him hadn't given her the opportunity to blow it out or curl it. She had complained, but he told her she looked beautiful with any hair style, coiffed or au naturel.

Victoria felt Quintin's mouth on her ear. He was as passionate and tender out of bed as he was in bed. A foreign emotion welled up within her and she felt tears prick the backs of her eyelids.

Shifting and pressing her lips to his, she whispered, "I love you so much, Quintin."

He stared down at the shadowy outline of her face. Lowering his head, he kissed her closed lids, catching the salty tears on the tip of his tongue.

"I was so afraid you wouldn't or couldn't love me," he confessed.

"It's so easy to love you," she retorted. "What I was afraid of was that you were in love with the woman I saw leaving your apartment a few weeks ago."

He pulled back, frowning. "What woman?"

"A woman who can claim a pair of stilts for legs."

Quintin remembered whom Victoria was referring to. "I don't get involved with models," he replied in a serious tone.

"You told me you'd met someone and—"

"That someone was *you,*" he interrupted. Quintin studied her bowed head, realization dawning quickly. "Is that why you wouldn't let me finish what we had begun earlier this morning?" She nodded, and Quintin laughed. "If we're going to have a normal relationship, Vicky Jones, then we're going to have to be honest with each other. No secrets. Okay?"

She smiled up him. "No secrets," she repeated.

Sixteen

Quintin's "I grew up in farm country" was confirmed as Victoria sat beside Quintin, staring out through the windshield at the passing countryside. They had left Baltimore's city limits twenty minutes before, and the landscape changed along with the sizes of the homes and surrounding properties. She noted the grazing cows, barns, horses, bales of hay, tractors, pickup trucks, and other farm vehicles behind fenced-off areas and along the shoulder of the road.

Quintin turned off a local two-lane road, shifted in four-wheel drive, and maneuvered up a rutted unpaved hill. Hannibal rose from his lounging position in the cargo area and barked excitedly.

"Hannibal!" Quintin admonished, glancing quickly over his shoulder and glaring at his pet. Hannibal sat down on his haunches, panting.

"He seems pretty excited," Victoria remarked, watching as a large white three-story house came into view. Several hundred feet of lush green lawn surrounded the house like a thick carpet.

"Watch him take off like a bullet as soon as I open the door," Quintin warned. "If Hannibal could talk he would call this 'Hannibal's Big Adventure.' "

"Somewhat like a kid going to Disney World?"

"Exactly," Quintin replied, laughing. "It'll take him a

week to recover from all of the attention he'll get from my nieces and nephews."

"He sounds like a real party animal." Quintin groaned at her pun, shaking his head. "I thought it was funny," Victoria retorted, managing to look insulted.

He slowed the Jeep, then parked. Leaning over, he pulled her from her seat and she lay half on and half off his chest and legs. Lowering his head, he pressed a tender kiss on her pouting mouth.

"I love you," he whispered, watching wonder light up her gaze. Every time he confessed his love to her it seemed as if it surprised her; it was as if she did not believe him.

Clutching his wrists, Victoria held on to Quintin, not wanting to let him go. The past twenty-four hours had been a time of discovery; it was as if she had discovered passion for the very first time in her life. A passion that was strong and spontaneous.

"I love you, too, darling."

Shifting slightly, she returned his kiss, her tongue sweeping over his mustached mouth.

Quintin jerked back as if he had been burned. "Do that again and I'll turn around and go back home," he threatened, grinning.

"And have your mother angry with me for keeping her son away from a family outing? I don't think so, Quintin Lord."

"I'd tell her I couldn't help it."

"Forget it."

He released her, shifted into gear and drove around the side of the large farmhouse where automobiles of every make and model were parked in rows of twos.

Quintin came around and helped Victoria from the four-wheeler, and she was met with a variety of tantalizing odors lingering in the warm late-spring air.

Hannibal sprang from the back of the Jeep as soon as

Quintin opened the cargo door, racing around to the back of the farmhouse.

A large white tent was erected under a copse of massive oak trees. Situated under the tent were two long wooden tables with benches crowded with adult couples, young adults, and a number of small children.

Victoria heard the words, "Quintin brought a girl" the moment gazes were turned in their direction.

"Hey, Quint," hooted Dwayne Lord. "Aren't you going to introduce us to your lady, or are you trying to keep her all to yourself."

"Wait your turn," Quintin warned his brother, steering Victoria toward his parents.

Etta Mae Lord greeted them warmly. She was a tall, gray-haired, large-boned woman without an ounce of excess fat. Her gold-brown eyes were bright and intelligent.

"Welcome." She held out her hands to Victoria.

"Thank you, Mrs. Lord." Victoria went into her embrace.

"Etta Mae," the older woman insisted.

"Etta Mae," Victoria repeated, hugging her in return.

The Lord matriarch assessed her son's date, nodding and smiling. It had taken Quintin too many years to count to bring a woman to a family celebration, but he had chosen wisely. The petite woman with the large dark eyes reminded Etta Mae of a fragile doll.

Victoria turned to Quintin's father who was only an inch taller than his dynamic wife. She was completely charmed by the gentle nature of Charles Lord. There was something about him that reminded her of Quintin.

After the introduction to Quintin's parents, Victoria met his brothers, sisters, nieces, nephews, and the fiancés, fiancées, boy and girlfriends of the single family members. Within minutes she was referred to as "Quintin's girlfriend."

Sharon Lord captured Victoria's arm, declaring she was

to be her hostess. "Quintin told me all about you," she confessed with a bright smile. "He said you took care of him when he had to have his wisdom tooth pulled."

She returned Sharon's smile. The resemblance between Sharon and her brother was startling. "He was a very good patient," Victoria confessed in all honesty.

"So it's not gratitude that made him bring you today?"

Victoria recalled their wonderful lovemaking, shaking her head. "I hope not."

"I hope not, either," Sharon said with a slight frown. But the expression disappeared as quickly as it formed. "I'm Hannibal's mother," she continued. "I'm a dog breeder, and Hannibal comes from a long line of pedigreed champion giant schnauzers."

"Do you show dogs or breed them?"

"Right now I'm just breeding them. But if I can convince Quintin to let me sire Hannibal to an exquisite pure black bitch schnauzer next month I'd be willing to train and show the best of their litter."

Victoria smiled as Quintin approached and handed her a glass of lemonade. "I'm willing to bet that my little sister is bending your ears about her dogs."

She took the glass. "Sharon was telling me that she wants to breed Hannibal."

Quintin curved an arm around Victoria's waist, winking at Sharon. "I have to ask Hannibal whether he's ready to become a papa."

"Once Onyx comes into heat he'll be ready," Sharon countered. "After all, he's a male, and aren't all males always ready to breed, dear brother? Are you blushing, Quintin Thomas Lord," she teased, peering up at him.

Quintin's mouth tightened under his mustache as he glared at his sister. "Are you hungry, Vicky?" Not waiting for her reply, he steered her in the direction of the tent.

Victoria leaned against his side, her breast pressing

against his arm. "She's right, darling. You're always ready."

Lowering his head, he whispered against her ear, "I have to be to keep up with you, sweetheart." Now it was Victoria's turn to feel the heat in her face. "I'll always be ready for you," he continued softly. "I'm ready now."

She looked up at him, her gaze registering the simmering passion lurking beneath his impassive expression. Her lips parted and she inhaled, feeling her breasts swell against the cotton fabric of her oversize T-shirt.

They could have been the only two people under the large tent as they were caught up in a dizzying spell of longing. Surreptitious glances were cast in their direction, conversations tapering off until there was complete silence. A young child whimpered and was quickly hushed by its mother.

Victoria was the first one to notice the strained silence, her gaze sweeping over the assembled guests. Unconsciously she moved closer to Quintin, and his arm tightened around her waist.

"I want Victoria on my team," he said smoothly, breaking the silence.

"No mixed teams this year," Lydia Lord reminded Quintin. At nineteen she was the youngest child of Charles and Etta Mae. "We decided last year that if you brought a girl it would be the girls against the guys."

Quintin shook his head. "I sure hate to see women cry."

"No more than I hate to hear men gnash their teeth." Lydia retorted, hands on hips.

Quintin released Victoria and made his way slowly toward Lydia. "Now why did you have to go there, Lydia? Why did you have to talk about teeth?"

Lydia sprinted out of his reach. "If the shoe fits, then wear it, Quintin Thomas Lord."

"The pig is ready," Charles Lord called out from outside of the tent, and everyone picked up a plate and made their way over to the pit where a whole pig had been roasting since before sunup.

The whole group was sprawled on the grass under trees, napping and relaxing after devouring mounds of potato salad, roast pork, barbecued chicken, cole slaw, and marinated vegetable salads. It would be another two hours before the annual baseball outing began. After the game everyone would sit down for dessert. Victoria had contributed to the dessert menu with three homemade sweet potato pies.

She sat on the ground under a tree, watching an infant crawl away from its mother in her direction. The barefoot little girl wore only a diaper and a sleeveless undershirt.

Victoria froze as the baby came closer, her heart pounding uncontrollably. Quintin was sprawled beside her, asleep.

The infant stopped and reached out with a tiny, chubby hand. The round dark eyes closed, filling with tears. A weak cry followed.

She felt the baby's frustration, but was paralyzed. She wanted to reach out and pick up the little girl, but her hands refused to follow the dictates of her brain.

Quintin came awake immediately. He glanced from his niece to Victoria. Sitting up, he picked up the infant and cradled her to his chest.

"Hey, hey, princess. It's all right," he crooned. The baby stopped crying, sniffling against his chest. He nestled her in the crook of his arm and placed a kiss on the tiny girl's forehead. "Uncle Quintin will take care of you."

Victoria watched in awe. The baby seemed to recognize her uncle's face and smiled, revealing four tiny white teeth.

"What's her name?" Her voice was low and breathless, and she was wary.

"Gabrielle."

"A beautiful name for a beautiful little girl."

Quintin handed Gabrielle to Victoria. "Hold her."

Victoria felt faint and her mouth seemed suddenly to be filled with cotton. *No, Quintin,* her head screamed. *I can't.*

"It's okay, Vicky. She won't cry." He thrust little Gabrielle at her and Victoria had no choice but to take her.

Gabrielle sensed Victoria's tension and began to fret again. "Don't cry. Please don't cry," she pleaded, trying to soothe the baby.

Gabrielle's whimpers turned to laughter, surprising Victoria. She smiled back at the tiny round brown face. "You are so adorable." The baby dropped her head to Victoria's chest and snuggled against her breasts.

The stiffness left her limbs, and she began to relax. Lowering her chin, she kissed the top of the baby's softly curling damp hair. Gabrielle had that clean smell exclusive only to a baby. She thrust a fist into her mouth and within seconds had fallen asleep.

Quintin moved closer to Victoria, dropping an arm over her shoulder. "What is it about you that children fall asleep in your arms? First Ryan and now Gabrielle. You remind me of the paintings of the Madonna with child."

She closed her eyes, not responding. He had no idea how difficult it was for her to hold a child, knowing every child she held would never be from her own body.

Richard's caustic words attacked her and she tightened her grip on Gabrielle's soft rounded body. *I want out of this marriage. Victoria. I need a woman who can give me children.* My *children, not someone else's throwaways.*

She shivered slightly as Quintin pressed his mouth to her ear, the silken hair on his upper lip sweeping over the sensitive flesh of her lobe.

"I want you so much," he whispered passionately. What

he didn't say was that he wanted her as his wife and the mother of his children.

Victoria smiled, not opening her eyes. He wanted her and she wanted him. She loved him and he loved her. At that moment life with Quintin was wonderful and perfect.

Victoria stood in a huddle with Quintin's three sisters, four sisters-in-law, and the girlfriend of his only single brother discussing strategy. All of the women wore black baseball caps with a large white L printed on the front.

"Victoria, you're new at this, so I need to warn you that the guys cheat," Sharon explained. "There's nothing too low or dirty they won't do in order to win. And that means they'll slide into you when you're covering a base, or whoever's going to be their catcher will block the plate even if he's not holding the ball." Her sherry-colored eyes glowed with excitement.

"We'll play three full innings, but if no one scores, then we'll play another three. Now, let's go out there and kick some booty!"

Victoria jogged out to second base. The expansive field in the back of the farmhouse had been turned into a baseball diamond many years ago. The grassy knoll beyond a low wooden fence some two hundred feet from home plate was designated as home-run territory. Lines of white chalk down the right and left fields outlined fair territory from foul.

Adjusting her cap and pounding her glove, Victoria leaned forward and concentrated on the first batter. She smiled. Quintin was the lead-off batter.

The annual Memorial Day baseball game had developed with some hard and fast rules: an underhand pitch was utilized with the larger softball along with the lighter weight aluminum bat, and Charles Lord stood behind the plate as the perennial umpire while Etta Mae kept score.

Teenage and preteen offspring sat on benches, cheering for their parents, aunts, and uncles.

Lydia went into her windup, and a wicked curve sailed close to Quintin's chin. He glared at her and crouched lower in his batting stance; he took the next pitch, but his bat made contact with the third one and it sailed over Victoria's head and out into center field. Sharon came up with the ball and threw it to Victoria a second after Quintin's foot made contact with the bag.

He smiled at Victoria. "Hi, beautiful." She ignored him, pounding her glove and watching as Quintin's oldest brother stepped into the batter's box.

Lydia, experienced with the masculine gender's strategy of taunting basemen, glanced over her shoulder. She lowered her head, watching as Quintin took a sizable lead toward third base. Without warning, she turned and fired the ball into second base. Victoria caught the perfect throw and tagged Quintin before he could lunge back to the bag.

"You're out!" Victoria screamed, leaning over a prone Quintin. He raised his head and glared at her. "Get off the field, handsome. You're holding up the game," she taunted.

"You'll pay for that," he threatened softly, rising to his feet and adjusting his cap.

"I can't wait."

He moved closer to her. "I'll make you beg."

"I can't wait," she repeated before he turned and loped off the playing field.

The game continued with no one scoring through the first three innings. The next three became intense as the women scored first with two back-to-back doubles in the bottom of the fifth inning. The men came back with two runs in the top of the sixth.

Sharon, Victoria, and Lydia were the scheduled batters for the bottom of the sixth inning. Sharon led off, exploding the first pitch over the fence at center field. All of the women gathered at home plate and waited while she circled the bases in a slow, victorious trot.

Play was resumed after the brief celebration. Victoria felt the tension as she gripped the bat and stepped into the batter's box. Moisture had formed between her breasts and ran in rivulets down her belly under the T-shirt. Her team had tied the score.

Dwayne went into his windup and pitched a missile past her chest. She stepped out of the box and inhaled deeply. Lydia's boyfriend pounded his glove loudly behind her. "Let's see another one just like that one, Dwayne!" the catcher shouted.

Dwayne complied, and the next pitch landed in the exact same spot. "Strike two," Charles intoned.

Victoria concentrated and crouched. The next pitch connected with the bat and sailed out into left field. She ran toward first base, her gaze on the ball. The left fielder lost the ball in the grass and she wound up on third base with a stand-up triple by the time it was relayed to the catcher.

"Nice hitting and nice base running," Quintin crooned behind her. "I was waiting for you to make it to third base all afternoon."

"Why?" she asked, not turning around.

"So I can do *this!*" Moving closer, he nuzzled the back of her neck.

"Quintin!" She remembered Sharon saying that the men would employ any trick to win.

"What would you do if I kissed you right now?"

"You can't interfere with the runner," she retorted. Lydia had stepped into the batter's box.

"I'm not interfering with the runner, Vicky. I just want to kiss my girlfriend."

Victoria took several steps up the third base line toward home plate. "I didn't know I was your girlfriend."

"You're more than my girlfriend," Quintin countered.

Victoria was not given an opportunity to ask what she was to Quintin because she was off and running as soon as Lydia's bat made contact with the ball. The shortstop fielded the ball and threw it to home plate.

Less than six feet from the plate, Victoria realized she was going to be out. The catcher was crouched to protect the plate and tag her. She increased her speed, springing and jumping over his head. She scrambled back and touched home plate just under his tag.

Charles Lord crossed his arms over the runner and catcher, shouting, "Safe!"

Seventeen

The victory celebration was loud and boisterous. Victoria was dubbed the female Ozzie Smith for her acrobatics on the playing field, and the members of her team lauded over, taunted, and jeered their male counterparts.

"Next year we're playing with mixed teams," Lucien Lord declared.

Lydia frowned at her oldest brother. "No way, Lucien. You guys just can't stand to lose. If you'd won you wouldn't be crying about having mixed teams."

"This is the first year we haven't had mixed teams," Lucien complained.

"And it won't be the first time the guys will lose, either," Sharon stated smugly.

"How were we to know that Quint's girlfriend was a gymnast," Dwayne grumbled, frowning.

"I'm not a gymnast," Victoria protested, unable to believe the men were so competitive.

"What are you?" every male member of the team chorused. Everyone except for Quintin. He leaned against a tree, arms folded over his chest, smiling.

"Tell them, Vicky," he urged.

She glared back at him. "I will not. Just because you lost doesn't mean the women should have to justify we have superior playing skills."

"You tell them, girlfriend," Lucien's wife shouted.

"Why can't you men accept defeat?" It was Etta Mae's

turn to bond with the winning female team. "You lost, gentlemen. Case closed."

"Dad . . . Dad, are you sure Victoria touched the bag before the tag?" Lucien would not concede defeat.

Charles Lord nodded slowly. "You lost, Son." His voice was soft and final.

Gloves and bats were gathered and placed in several large plastic milk crates. The annual Memorial Day baseball competition was over until the next year.

Everyone filed into the farmhouse and waited in turn to use the two and a half bathrooms there to wash up before sitting down to enjoy dessert.

"Who made the potato pie?" the female voice shouted to be heard above the din in the large kitchen. "Etta Mae, did you make the pie?"

"Not me," Etta Mae replied.

Sharon took a bite of her slice of sweet potato pie. "This is not Mama's pie. Who made the pie?"

Quintin, sitting beside Victoria at a large oak table, stared at Victoria's impassive profile. She was not going to admit she had baked the pie.

Gabrielle's mother cradled the baby on her hip while cutting a small piece of pie from her husband's plate. "Are you sure this isn't your pie, Etta Mae?"

"Even if I could make the filling as creamy and spicy as this, I've never been able to roll out my crusts this thin," Etta Mae confessed.

Lydia nodded. "Mama's right. This is not her crust."

"Who made the potato pie?" Lucien's fifteen-year-old son walked into the kitchen, his mouth full.

"Weasel out of this one," Quintin whispered close to Victoria's ear.

She glared at him, eyes narrowing. "You better not say anything." Her voice was low and threatening.

"Mama, Vicky's threatening me," he wailed, concealing a grin.

"Grow up, Quintin," Etta Mae admonished.

Quintin's grin grew wider. "She's threatening to beat me up if I tell that she made the sweet potato pies."

There was a stunned silence, everyone's gaze fixed on her flushed face.

"What *don't* you do well?" Sharon questioned, glancing from Victoria to her brother.

"She's perfect," Quintin announced proudly.

"You've got that right," Dwayne confirmed under his breath. He earned a solid punch to his shoulder from his girlfriend for his comment.

Victoria was besieged with questions about how she made her crust and what ingredients she added to the mashed sweet potatoes to achieve its distinctive taste. It wasn't until half an hour later that she escaped to the outdoors.

The air had cooled down considerably with the setting sun as she made her way across the front lawn. Many of the young adults and small children sat on the grass in groups of twos and threes, talking or arguing softly and cheerfully. A few of them called out to her as she passed, and she acknowledged them with a smile and a wave.

The Lords were a dynamic and somewhat overpowering family. She wasn't used to the noise and energy they seemed to expend effortlessly.

Charles and Etta Mae were not only tolerant, but they were proud of their children and grandchildren. There was no mistaking their pride with the fun-loving, good-natured family unit.

"Victoria, may I talk to you?"

She turned, smiling at an excited Lydia. "Of course."

The nineteen-year-old was tall and willowy as a young sapling. The only feature she shared with Quintin was her eyes. They were the same gold-brown shade and were framed by long thick lashes.

"I'd like to ask a favor," Lydia began shyly.

Victoria smiled, trying to put the young woman at ease. "Ask."

"I'd like to work with you. What I mean is, will you teach me to cook . . . prepare certain dishes. I'm majoring in culinary arts with a minor in restaurant and hotel management. I just completed my first year," she rushed on, "and I'd love to get some hands-on experience."

"Are you working now?"

Lydia shook her head. "I've applied to several restaurants, but no one has hired me. I've told them I'll do anything. Wait or bus tables. Even wash dishes. But everyone that I've spoken to said they don't want to train me, then have me leave when classes begin again in the fall. I want experience, Victoria. Nothing else."

Victoria was charmed by Lydia's enthusiasm. She was older than Lydia when she decided on a career in the culinary arts, and her own enthusiasm had been similar.

Her business enterprise was in its infancy stage. She knew it would be only a matter of time before she'd need an assistant. An assistant she would have to train, and one she could depend on.

"Do you attend a local college?"

"Yes."

"Will you be available on weekends during the school year?"

"Yes."

A slight frown appeared between her eyes as she considered Lydia's proposal. "I can't pay you much—"

I don't want any pay," Lydia interrupted.

Victoria smiled, shaking her head. "Okay. Can you start tomorrow morning?"

"Yes, yes, yes!" Lydia clenched her hands, then bit down on her lower lip.

"Be at my place tomorrow at ten o'clock."

Lydia lowered her hands and took a deep breath. "Where do you live?"

"Next door to your brother. I'm his neighbor."

When Lydia squealed, several people turned and glanced over at her. "I don't believe it. Lucky for you, Victoria. As Sharon would put it, 'You've got the pick of the Lord litter.' Both Sharon and I agree that Quintin is our favorite brother. He always spoiled us and we're *very* protective of him."

Victoria smiled. "You think Quintin needs protecting?"

"Not really," she confessed. "It's just that I've always thought Quintin is very special. He wasn't anything like my other brothers who forced every guy who got up enough nerve to date my sisters to run a fierce gauntlet."

Victoria thought of her own brother's reaction when he found out that Richard had asked her out. Richard had to reassure Nat that he had no intention of sleeping with his sister unless they were married.

"What did they do?" she asked Lydia.

"They usually met them at the door and described in detail a slow form of dismemberment, starting with the fingers, if they even remotely entertained the notion of seducing their sisters. It took a while before the word got out that they were bluffing."

She couldn't help herself as she burst out laughing. Lydia curved an arm around her shoulders and hugged her.

"Thank you again. I'll see you tomorrow morning."

Lydia returned to the house and Quintin watched Victoria as she stared at his sister's retreating figure. He hadn't been able to talk Lydia out of approaching Victoria about becoming her apprentice. He didn't want her to feel obligated to hire his sister because of their relationship. Thinking of sleeping together, he couldn't wait to be alone with her again.

He made his way over to Victoria, his step light, his

stride loose and fluid. Curving an arm around her waist, he led her away from the house.

"Did you hire her?"

Victoria wound her left arm around Quintin's waist. "Yes."

"You didn't have to." His voice was low and soothing.

"I know I didn't."

"Don't let her get away with—"

"Don't worry, Quintin," she cut in. "I'm not going to coddle her. She'll work and work hard. Lydia will only be successful if she's serious about wanting to become a chef."

Pulling her closer, Quintin leaned over and kissed her forehead. "Good."

"And I'll not tolerate any interference from you if I have to reprimand her."

Stopping, he turned to face her. "I will not interfere. You have my word on that."

Victoria's wide-eyed gaze was fixed on his face, taking in everything that was Quintin Lord and everything about him that permitted her to love him so freely.

She smiled up at him, leaning toward his tall, strong body. "I'm glad I came today. I've had a lot of fun."

Quintin's hands cradled her upturned face. "I'm sure you and the ladies had a lot of fun kicking the stuffing out of the Lords with that little ballet maneuver. You're lucky I didn't tell the Lords that you were a dancer."

Her fingers went to his strong wrists. "You act as if I did something illegal, Quintin. Major-league ballplayers go through ballet maneuvers as a part of their physical training."

"We're not major-league ballplayers."

"I can see that. But maybe if the Lords were professional players they would learn how to lose without moaning and pouting. Why is it so hard to admit the ladies beat you?"

His eyes narrowed in intensity. "Because we're very

competitive," he stated, his voice taking on a serious tone. Lowering his hands, he grasped her hand and led her out to the grassy baseball field.

"What you've seen today is what every male Lord had to experience when growing up," he began. "My mother gave birth to nine children over a span of twenty-two years. Some of us were only eleven months apart, others two years, and the next child always had to fight for attention and independence. My sisters had it a lot easier. They've grown up protected and indulged by everyone. Therefore, they are a lot less competitive."

Victoria concentrated on placing one foot in front of the other. "Are you saying that you didn't have a happy childhood?"

Quintin stopped and shook his head. "No, Vicky. I had the best childhood anyone could ask for. I was wanted, loved, provided for, and encouraged to be whatever I wanted to be. I knew I wanted to be an artist since I was about ten and my father paid for my art lessons. There was never a question that he wouldn't agree to do it."

Squeezing her fingers gently, he continued walking. "I suppose we get our competitiveness from Etta Mae. This land belonged to her family. Her great-grandfather bought three acres of farmland, raising a breed of cattle that were resistant to most diseases while yielding lean tender meat.

"As his profits increased he bought up more adjacent lands until he and his brothers had a small empire of nearly a thousand beef and milk cows spread out over more than six hundred acres. By the time he'd educated his children and grandchildren the family's interest in breeding livestock dwindled until the land was sold off in large parcels. All that is left is ten acres."

There was a quiet, comfortable silence as they made their way over the land on which thousands of hooves had trampled. Ancient trees, with massive trunks and sweeping branches, broke up the monotony of grassland. Quintin sat down under one of the trees, pulling Victoria down with him.

Easing her back to the grass, he smiled down at her, running a forefinger over her nose and down to her lips.

"I've wanted to do this all day," he confessed seconds before he covered her mouth with his.

She felt the comforting crush of his weight as he covered her body, reveling in the taste of his mouth and his strength. Her ardor rose quickly and her fingers gathered the fabric of his T-shirt, pulling it up where she kneaded the hard muscles in his broad back. Her breath rushed out between her lips in short gasps.

She wanted him! The gush of wetness between her thighs startled her. His touch, his kiss, was enough to make her ready for him.

But she couldn't make love to him now. Not on the ground, and not where someone could discover them.

"Quintin, please," she moaned as his tongue plunged recklessly into her mouth.

Quintin's right hand searched under her T-shirt, capturing a firm, ripe breast, and, without warning, his mouth replaced his hand. She arched, keening, pushing the distended nipple farther into his mouth.

"Quintin, no!" The nipple slipped from between his teeth, his head coming up, and Victoria saw something in the depths of the gold-brown gaze she had never seen before. There was passion but there was also an expression of fevered abandonment. A heated frenzy lurking just below the surface, ready to ravish her mind as well as her body.

Closing her eyes, she pulled down her shirt. "Let's go back," she said hoarsely.

Rolling off her body, Quintin came to his feet and extended his hand. "Let's go *home*."

Eighteen

"My place or yours?" Victoria asked, opening the front door. Quintin followed her down the hall to their apartments.

"Mine," he replied.

"Let me get something to change into and I'll be right over."

Quintin pulled her against his body. "You don't need clothes."

"I'm not going to walk around naked," she protested.

"I like you naked," he countered, grinning.

"You're an animal." Her tone was a teasing one.

He pressed a light kiss to her mouth. "Wrong, Vicky. Hannibal's the animal, and even he's going to have his share of fun for the next few weeks."

Quintin had given in to Sharon's plea that he permit her to breed Hannibal with her prized Onyx. Hannibal would spend the next two weeks with Onyx before the bitch came into heat, hopefully with successful results.

Victoria opened the door and made her way into her apartment. She'd left the air-conditioning on and the high-ceilinged spaces were cool and refreshing.

It took less than fifteen minutes to check her answering machine and gather a change of clothes and her personal toiletries. A message from Jo confirmed that Sunny Calhoun wanted VJ Catering to provide the food for her upcoming Wednesday afternoon luncheon, and the call from

Ethan Bennington asked that she call him Tuesday morning at nine-thirty. He left the number to the Greater Baltimore Cultural Center before the message ended.

The throbbing rendition of Percy Sledge's "When A Man Loves a Woman" flowed from hidden speakers as she walked through the open door to Quintin's apartment.

A slight smile softened Victoria's mouth. His apartment was immaculate, verifying his claim that he had hired a cleaning woman.

"You're just in time. I filled the tub for your bath." Quintin came down the staircase wearing only a pair of cut-off jeans. He slung a damp towel around his neck.

Victoria smiled up at him. It hadn't taken Quintin long to recognize her routine. She always showered in the morning, but preferred a leisurely bath before going to bed.

"Tonight you're in for a real treat. I'm going to give you a massage."

"I can't wait," she crooned, winking saucily and moving past him up the staircase.

Victoria lay facedown on the bed. Quintin knelt over her and gently kneaded her calves and the backs of her thighs. His strong fingers had dissolved the knotted muscles in her neck and shoulders, then worked their magic down her back to her legs.

The pungent fragrance of her body cream lingered in the air as she gave in to his expert touch, moaning sensually. She was so relaxed, Quintin had to repeat his query.

"No, you're not hurting me," she slurred.

Lowering his chest to her back, he covered her body, supporting most of his weight on his elbows. "You have an exquisite body, Vicky. I'd love to paint you in the nude."

She froze, her eyes opening. "No."

"The painting would only be for me," he whispered

against her ear. "It would become a part of my private collection."

"You have a private collection?"

Quintin nodded. The picture of her on her patio was nearly completed. It was the first of many he intended to paint with Victoria as his model.

"How many paintings do you have in your private collection?"

"Just one."

"Is it a nude?"

"No. The subject is clothed."

Victoria swallowed loudly. She wasn't a prude, but she never considered sitting for a portrait—especially not a nude.

Quintin rolled off her body and pulled her to his side. His gaze was fixed on her mouth. "I don't want frontal nudity. I'd have you sit on a chair in profile, one leg draped over the other. The focus would be on your legs and feet. Your arms would be crossed over your breasts with your hands cupping your elbows. Your head would be tilted back, showing off the curve and length of your neck and the fragile bones of your jawline. I'd paint you from the left side because that's your best angle."

She was flattered her wanted to paint her, but she didn't feel comfortable knowing anyone would be able to view her nude body.

"I'm sorry, Quintin. I can't. I—"

"That's all right, darling," he interrupted. "Forget I asked."

The fingers of his right hand lifted several strands of hair from over her ear, his touch as light as the brush of a butterfly's wing. A slight smile lifted the corners of his mouth under his mustache.

"What are you staring at?" she asked, capturing his gaze with her own.

"You."

The heat rose in her cheeks. "Why?" Her voice had dropped an octave.

"Because I like looking at you."

"Do you like what you see?"

His lids came down slowly as his grin widened. "Very much."

She returned his smile. "I'm glad."

His hand moved from her hair, down to a bare shoulder, and still lower to her waist, pulling her to his body until her bare breasts were flattened against his chest. His warm breath filtered over her mouth.

"Don't move. There's one thing I forgot to do to you."

Victoria lay on her back, staring up at the ceiling. Never had she felt so loved, so adored and pampered.

Quintin returned, sitting down on the side of the bed. A slight smile played at the corners of his sensual mouth. "I have to fluff you up."

She jerked, not knowing whether to laugh or turn away in shame. Quintin wielded a small comb, the teeth moving tentatively over the thick, dark tangled hair between her thighs.

He shifted his eyebrows as a full grin creased his face. "Now, it looks very nice. Take a look, Vicky. See how fluffy it is."

She half rose, cheeks filled with fire, surveying his handiwork. "Nice," she managed to croak.

"How do you taste, Vicky?"

Closing her eyes against his intense penetrating stare, she shook her head. "I don't know."

Quintin's hands moved up her thighs, cupping her hips. "You've never been tasted before?"

"No," she shuddered, visibly shaken by his erotic questioning.

She hadn't lied. Richard was the first man she'd slept with, and their lovemaking had been satisfying. Richard had been experienced, but he had also been very traditional.

"Do you want me to tell you how you taste?"

She sat up, her fingers catching in the hair on his chest. She was unable to hide their trembling from Quintin. She wanted him!

For the second time that day he had her aching and trembling for him.

"Do you?" he repeated.

Hiding her face in his throat, Victoria inhaled the cleanliness of his flesh, savoring the masculine smell of his freshly showered body.

Every nerve in her body tightened and screamed with desire. She ached with unleashed passion.

"Yes." The single word was a tortured moan.

Holding on to her, Quintin reached out and dimmed the lamp. If he was going to introduce Victoria to another level of sensuality, then he had to put her at ease.

He knew inherently that Victoria Jones was capable of grand passion, and he wanted to be the one to unleash that passion. He wanted to wipe away the memory of any man who had claimed her before. He wanted to be the last lover in her life.

He wanted her to want him as much as he wanted her, and he wanted her to want him in her life until they both ceased to exist.

"Relax, baby," he crooned, smoothing her hair off her face and easing her back down to the bed. "Let me do all of the work."

Closing her eyes, Victoria let her senses take over. She heard Quintin remove his cut-off jeans and drop them to the floor. She felt him move over her body, his greater weight comforting and protective.

"Stay with me, Vicky."

She nodded, not opening her eyes. She moaned once as his mustached mouth sought out her exposed throat. The brush of the hair on his upper lip over her throat was startling. The sensation of his mustache against her silken flesh intensified as he moved down her chest.

Her hands curled into tight fists. His tongue on her breasts, coating them with moisture, beaded the areola and brought her nipples into instant prominence. He alternated licking them with blowing his breath and rolling the swollen nipple between his teeth. She cried out once, but then bit down on her lower lip to stop any further sound.

"That was very good," he murmured, inching down her body.

Victoria's legs were trembling uncontrollably by the time he explored her flat belly. She went rigid when his hot breath seared the furred triangle between her thighs.

Sliding down the bed, Quintin gently forced her legs apart. He heard her first gasp of shock, but it was lost in the ensuing sobs of passion as his mouth worked its magic.

Writhing, Victoria couldn't stop her hips from moving as her body vibrated with liquid fire.

Her rising passion threatened to consume her before she reached fulfillment, and that fulfillment was poised, teasing, and hypnotic. She felt the hysteria of delight radiating from every pressure point in her body while her nerve endings screamed relentlessly.

Her head thrashed back and forth on the pillow and a cry was torn from the back of her throat.

"Quintin!"

He registered her desperation, her fear, and he acknowledged his own burning, pressing need to bury himself in her body.

Moving fluidly up her trembling form, he entered her in one smooth strong thrust of possession.

His own breath was coming quickly through parted lips. He felt her warm, wet, throbbing flesh close around him and he trembled uncontrollably.

Victoria was pulling and sucking him in. He didn't know where she began and he ended. Her legs encircled his waist, allowing him deeper access. She was driving him crazy. But if he was going to lose his mind he wanted her with him.

Victoria felt every muscle in Quintin's upper body straining; she heard his deep, labored breathing; she felt the dizzying pumping of his heart against her breasts, and she savored every strong thrust of his hips against hers.

She found his mouth and tasted herself on his lips. A moan of ecstasy escaped her when his large hands slipped under her hips, holding her tightly as he drove into her with a frenzied pumping motion.

She soared higher and higher until she exploded in a shower of shivering delight, whispering his name over and over. Before her sighs of completion faded, Quintin's unrestrained cry of passion filled the room.

He collapsed heavily on her body, gasping for air, reversing their positions. Victoria rested her cheek on his damp chest, trembling uncontrollably.

Quintin's breathing slowed and her trembling subsided, then stilled. Both of them were smiling broadly.

"Quintin?"

"Hmm-mm?"

"How did I taste?"

He opened one eye, peering down at her upturned face. Her smile was that of a completely satisfied woman. Lifting a shoulder, he shifted his eyebrows. "I suppose it was all right." He pulled a sheet up over their moist bodies.

Her face burned in embarrassment. She should've never asked. He didn't like it.

"You were delicious," he admitted after a lengthy silence.

Victoria wanted to punch him for teasing her. Shifting to face him, she pressed a kiss to his hard shoulder.

Without warning, she went rigid. "Quintin?"

"What is it?" He sat up suddenly.

"There's a furry animal in the bed." Her voice was a strained whisper.

Quintin pulled back the sheet, searching the large bed. "Where, Victoria? Where is it?" he repeated, fearful that maybe a rodent had gotten into the house.

Victoria moved quickly to his side, her right hand searching between his thighs. "Here it is," she said, cradling his sex in her splayed fingers.

He stared down at her hand as realization dawned. She was only teasing.

All levity waned quickly when he grew hard and heavy in her hand. Their gazes met and locked. Rising to her knees, Victoria curled into the curve of his body and kissed him deeply.

"I love you," she confessed seconds before he eased her back to the pillows.

"Not as much as I love you," he rasped, devouring her mouth and demonstrating the depth of his feelings for her.

He didn't ask the question that plagued his every waking moment. He couldn't wait until he felt the time was right to ask Victoria Jones to become his wife.

Victoria led Lydia Lord into the kitchen five minutes before ten o'clock. Lydia had arrived early. That was a good sign. The young woman would be punctual and dependable.

"I'll show you where everything is, but first I want to show you my calendar for the next week." A large calendar indicating three months at a glance was filled with notations.

"I have a new client," Victoria began. "Mrs. Calhoun holds a weekly Wednesday luncheon for about a dozen women, ranging in age from the mid-fifties to late sixties. I always consider age when preparing a menu. I'm certain these women are watching their weight as well as blood pressure and cholesterol readings.

"And that means I'll prepare low-fat, low-sodium, and high-fiber dishes. But that doesn't mean that the dishes won't be attractive or palatable."

Lydia studied the calendar. "What will you serve for her luncheon tomorrow?"

"I'm considering a spiced chicken salad over shredded lettuce, sliced cucumber, and tomatoes. The chicken stays moist and full of flavor because it's prepared in a yogurt marinade. There's another salad known as a Wensleydale salad. It's made with shredded white cabbage, red pepper, Wensleydale cheese, thinly sliced scallions, and black olives. The dressing is a mixture of plain yogurt, coarse-grained mustard, and honey."

"That sounds fabulous."

"Any cheese I use will be a low-fat. Then there's always a summer green salad of romaine, oak leaf, dandelion, or sorrel leaves. Sometimes I add very young and tender spinach leaves."

Lydia's dark eyes glittered with excitement. "What about the entrèe?"

"Most likely shrimp creole with a rice pilaf. But for those who cannot eat shellfish, I'll offer a grilled chicken breast with the pilaf."

"Dessert?"

"Peaches cardinale, a summer fruit compote, or gelato."

"Sounds delicious. Now let's go shopping. I have to prepare for an anniversary celebration this coming weekend. I want to show you how I select different cuts of meat. Our first stop will be a wholesale butcher."

Victoria spent the better part of an hour showing Lydia her kitchen and explaining what pots and what utensils were used for the preparation and cooking of certain dishes. The young woman was a quick study, jotting down notes in a small binder.

Watching Lydia's hands as she made a notation, Victoria frowned. "You're going to have to cut your nails."

Lydia's head came up quickly, then her gaze shifted to her long, delicate fingers. Her nails were long and shimmered with a bright red color.

"No polish, either," she continued. "No one wants to see flecks of red on their freshly whipped cream or eat particles of uncooked meat or poultry with their fresh lettuce leaves from the residue left under your nails."

Lydia nodded. "Do you have a nail clipper, polish remover, and an emery board?"

Victoria patted the younger woman's shoulder in a comforting gesture. "Come with me."

She had heard the same lecture the first day she attended classes at the culinary school in Washington, D.C. The instructor had listed the do's and don't's on a chalkboard, and long fingernails headed the list of don't's.

One of her male classmates teased her relentlessly, dubbing her "Sally Hansen" until she beat him out for first prize during a pastry-making competition. That was the beginning of many awards she garnered before winning a full graduate scholarship to attend the La Varenne École de Cuisine in France.

"You're going to be very good," she told Lydia after she had clipped, stripped, and filed her beautiful nails."

Lydia managed a strained smile. "How do you know that?"

"Because you want to be successful, Lydia. And you have enough Lord competitiveness in you to make sacrifices in order to achieve that success."

"Thank you for believing in me, Victoria."

She wanted to ask Victoria whether she was aware that they were to become family in the very near future. Both she and Sharon agreed that Quintin was in love with Victoria, and the possessive look in his eyes indicated he would not let her go without a battle. The look was a familiar one. All of the Lord brothers had had a similar look just before they asked the woman they had fallen in love with to marry them.

"Let's get busy," Victoria said, picking up her own notebook filled with items she had to order for a very busy week of cooking and baking.

Nineteen

Victoria and Lydia spent the morning and early afternoon selecting cuts of beef, lamb, smoked and fresh hams, and poultry from a wholesale meat packer. The butcher wrote down her explicit instructions as to how she wanted the meats dressed and when they should be delivered. Lydia stood by, watching and listening intently.

When they returned to the minivan, Victoria headed straight for the fish market. "There will come a time when all I'll need to do is call in my order to the butcher and he'll know how I want the meat cut and dressed."

"What about the fish people?" Lydia asked.

"I'll pick up the fish because it's a lot easier to buy and prepare."

Lydia stared out through the windshield, her brow furrowed in concentration. "It seems as if there's so much to learn."

"It appears that way in the beginning. I never thought I would learn the differences between all of the salad greens," Victoria admitted. "There's arugula, Belgium Endive, and Wirloof. Then there's Bibb, Boston, and iceberg lettuce. Cabbage comes in red, green, ruffly savoy, and Chinese. And you must remember that Belgium endive or Wirloof taste different from the bitter-tasting curly, flattened heads of regular chicory or endive. Dandelion, escarole, romaine, watercress, and spinach are also seen in many of today's salads."

"What would you prepare if you were cooking for vegetarians?" Lydia questioned.

"I'd steam my vegetables or blanch them and use them in a salad."

Lydia continued questioning Victoria, eager to learn.

"What vegetables would you use?"

"Cucumbers, red and green bell peppers, red and white radish, all varieties of tomatoes, scallions, asparagus, green and wax beans, broccoli, cauliflower, carrots, celery, white turnips, kohlrabi, snow peas, zucchini, mushrooms, red and Spanish onion, fennel and bean sprouts," Victoria paused. "The list is endless. Fruit salads can also be used to satisfy vegetarians as well as those who eat meat."

She glanced at Lydia's profile. "Ready to quit?"

"No," Lydia replied quickly. "Someday I want to own a gourmet, four-star restaurant."

Victoria nodded, remembering the different stations she covered while learning the restaurant business. Before she worked her way up to sous chef she had worked at the grill, sauté, pasta, and pastry stations. She demonstrated remarkable skill as a garde manager when she supervised all cold food preparation, including sandwiches and salads. Preparing elaborate salads had become her specialty.

The two women spent less than fifteen minutes selecting large succulent shrimp for the creole and a half-dozen softshell crabs for their dinner later that evening.

On the return trip home Lydia was quiet, reviewing the notes in her small binder while Victoria's thoughts were of Quintin.

They had made love again earlier that morning just as the sun rose to herald the beginning of a new day. After their pulses slowed and their breathing returned to normal, they lay together, limbs entwined and hearts beating as one.

Quintin had whispered over and over that he loved her; loved her more than he had ever thought it possible he could love any woman. She registered the deep passion in his voice and cried silently. He comforted her, believing her tears were an expression of joy. He never knew of her fear; a fear that he would want something from her that she was unable to offer him.

Lydia sat between her brother and Victoria on the patio devouring soft-shell crab sandwiches with red-pepper mayonnaise, a salad of mixed greens with sun-dried tomatoes in a honey-mustard sauce, iced tea made with a refreshing bubbly seltzer, and several scoops of hazelnut gelato.

"Do you eat like this every day, Quintin?" Lydia asked.

"Just about," he admitted, dabbing his mouth with a cloth napkin.

Lydia shook her head. "It's like dying and going to heaven."

Flashing a smile, Quintin stared at Victoria. "I die and go to heaven every time Vicky and I . . ." He broke off quickly when he realized what he was about to say. Lowering his gaze, he grimaced as both women stared at him.

"When you and Vicky do what, my darling brother?" Lydia teased.

Not bothering to answer, Quintin stood up and began clearing the table. Victoria and Lydia stared at his retreating back, then burst out laughing, the sound following him into the apartment.

They sobered, then Lydia offered to help clean up. Victoria refused, saying, "You'd better call it a day. You have a lot to digest before you come back tomorrow. If you get here around eight I'll have you help me prepare the dishes for the Calhoun luncheon. You'll only work half a day tomorrow, because you're going to need all of your energy for Thursday and Friday. You'll probably be on your feet each day for about six to eight hours."

Lydia nodded. Lowering her chin, she smiled shyly. "Can I have another serving of gelato before I leave?"

"I'll give you some to take home."

Lydia was overjoyed when she was given the choice of choosing the flavors. She selected a quart of mascarpone and zabaglione.

"Good choice," Quintin said, smiling at his youngest sister.

"You've tasted these?" she asked him.

Crossing his arms over his chest, he nodded slowly. "I've had the extreme pleasure of tasting *every* flavor."

Lydia stared at his flat midsection. "Be careful. You know how hard it is to keep your weight down as you get older."

"Go home, fresh mouth!" His smile belied his sharp tone.

"I'm going, I'm going," Lydia whispered, walking on tiptoe across the kitchen, carrying a bag with the gelato.

Victoria and Quintin, arm-in-arm, followed Lydia to the outer door. They watched as she settled herself behind the wheel of her Honda Civic, and waved to her as she drove off. She returned their wave through an open window.

Quintin pulled Victoria against his side. "How was she?"

"She's good, Quintin." Turning in his embrace, Victoria smiled up at him. "Let's go for a walk."

Quintin nodded. He returned to his apartment to get his keys. Minutes later, he and Victoria walked outside together enjoying the warmth of the twilight and smiling at other couples who had decided to take advantage of the warm evening.

They walked for a mile in silence before retracing their steps. As they neared their block, Quintin broke the silence saying, "I'm not going to be able to see as much of you in the next few weeks as I'd like. I have to do a shoot of a clothing designer's latest creations. If I can get the project completed in three weeks I'll be lucky."

She squeezed his fingers. "That's not going to be a problem because my calendar is also filling up."

He stopped and cradled her face between his hands, exhaling audibly. "When I do a shoot I really get wrapped up in my work, and I just don't want you to think that I'm avoiding or ignoring you."

"Don't worry about me, Quintin. I'm a lot more secure than you think." At that moment she was, not knowing that her statement soon would be replayed in her head, over and over, haunting her relentlessly.

Quintin slipped from Victoria's bed two hours before dawn, brushing a light kiss across her soft lips. "I'll see you later tonight," he promised.

He kissed her again and reached for his jeans. Making his way down the staircase, he walked out of her apartment and into his own.

An unexplainable shiver of apprehension swept through him as he walked into the bathroom. He went through the unconscious motion of shaving, looking at his reflection staring back at him in the mirror.

He hadn't made love to Victoria either the night before or that morning. She hadn't asked him to nor had she intimated that she wanted to be intimate with him. She seemed content to lie beside him, one leg draped over his thigh. She had been unusually quiet, and instead of trying to draw her out, he permitted her to withdraw from him. And when he left her bed he somehow felt her withdrawal was complete.

Showering and dressing quickly, he loaded his cameras, canisters of film, and tripod into the Jeep. He drove down quiet streets, heading east toward the ocean. Streaks of pink and pale blue were just beginning to brighten the sky as he pulled into a parking area along a stretch of sandy beach.

Four tall, emaciated-looking models stood on the sand, clutching cups of steaming liquids and pouting. Their bodies were swaddled in flowing robes and caftans. Quintin nodded after he gave them a quick glance, then began setting up his equipment.

He recognized the preening divas. Each one thought she was more beautiful and more photogenic than the other. He found them too thin, too vain, and much too superficial; however, behind the camera lens they were transformed into delicate, colorful butterflies and peacocks.

A slight smile softened his mouth. He much preferred Victoria Jones's looks. She was soft and totally feminine. Her face was enchanting, her body sensual, and her legs perfect. He found it hard to believe she had come into his life, filling a void he didn't known existed.

Checking the light with a meter, he adjusted the lens on the camera positioned atop the tripod. In another ten minutes there would be enough light to begin photographing.

He signaled the director, and a short, slightly built man dressed in white waved his hands at the sullen women.

"Ladies, ladies. We're ready." His voice carried easily over the soft lapping waves.

In unison, cover-ups were discarded. The wardrobe mistress took them and disappeared into a tent a short distance down the beach.

The models were dressed in colorful wraparound skirts in a Ghanaian cloth. The skirts revealed flat stomachs, hipbones, and inverted belly buttons. A half dozen strands of large Moroccan beads hung from long, thin necks, modestly covering four pairs of small brown breasts.

Quintin checked the light again. The rising sun cast a golden shield behind the women, turning their varying shades of brown skin into pearlized satin.

Peering through the camera lens, Quintin motioned with his right hand. "Ryanna, show me more of your right shoulder. That's it. Vashit, raise your chin just a tad. Good," he crooned.

The four women raised sticklike arms covered with circles of brass and wood, and posed—lips pouting, eyes hooded, bare feet arched. Their narrow bodies swayed to the sounds of drums coming from the speakers of the large portable tape player next to the dress designer.

Satisfaction lit up the face of Abayomi Koffigoh as she watched the models come alive in front of the camera. Business was good enough for her to hire top models to show off her latest creations, and good enough for her to hire one of the best photographers to shoot them.

Her dark eyes narrowed behind the lenses of her sunglasses. When she had interviewed Quintin Lord for the assignment he was friendly yet very businesslike. He ignored her veiled attempt to attend a dinner party at her home and she had shrugged off his refusal. He probably didn't like women, she had mused.

Quintin used two rolls of film before the models retreated to the tent to change into their next outfit. He shot another six rolls before the sun bore mercilessly down on the women's exposed skin and the director decided to wrap up the shoot for the day. Weather permitting, they all agreed to meet the following morning for more beach scenes.

"If you want me here tomorrow somebody had better do something with my hair," screamed one of the models.

Without turning around Quintin knew the strident voice belonged to the quixotic Alicia Sherwood. The exquisitely photogenic woman always left her calling card whenever he shot her at his apartment: a delicate scrap of underwear.

"What's wrong with your hair?" Abayomi asked.

Alicia waved a delicate hand. "These braids are pulling

my eyes up without the aid of cosmetic surgery. In other words, they're too damned tight."

Abayomi managed a saccharine grin, successfully concealing her rising annoyance with the temperamental model. "I'll make certain your hair is rebraided."

"Thanks," Alicia drawled, her large eyes fixed on Quintin's back. "See you tomorrow, Quintin," she crooned.

He turned around and graced her with a warm smile. "Alicia." Turning again, he picked up the leather bag with his equipment and slung it over his shoulder while grasping the tripod in his free hand. He headed back to the parking lot. The next four to six hours would be spent in the darkroom in his apartment, developing the film and making up contact sheets. Then later that evening he would see Victoria.

Just knowing he would see her made the day spent away from her worthwhile.

Twenty

Victoria sat across the table in her dining room, her chin resting on the heel of one hand, staring at Ethan Bennington's lowered head. The luncheon dishes she'd served Mrs. Calhoun and her guests that afternoon had been an unqualified success, and the dinner meeting with Ethan promised more success for VJ Catering. He wanted her to cater the cultural center's fifth anniversary celebration.

Ethan scrawled his signature across the bottom of a check. "This should cover the cost of the food and your services," he said, handing her the check. "If it's not enough please let me know."

She stared at the amount. The check drawn on his personal account far exceeded the amount she'd need to purchase, prepare, and serve food for the confirmed two hundred invited guests.

Placing the check, facedown, on the table, Victoria smiled. "It's enough, Ethan."

"I . . ." Whatever he was going to say was interrupted by the chiming of the doorbell. He rose to his feet as Victoria pushed back her chair.

"Please excuse me."

When she opened the door it was to find Quintin standing in the doorway, smiling down at her.

"Hey," he said softly.

"Hey yourself," she countered, taking his hand and pulling him into the entryway. "You're just in time to see your friend before he leaves."

Quintin tightened his grip on her fingers, pulling her back. "What friend?"

She urged him forward. "Come and see."

He followed her to the dining room, his mouth tightening noticeably when he saw Ethan rise to his feet, extending his hand. "What's up, buddy?"

That's what I want to know, he thought angrily. What the hell was Ethan doing in Victoria's apartment? Why was he eating at her table?

There was only a pulse beat of hesitation before Quintin extended his hand. "Not much. What's up with you?"

"I'm trying to pull everything together for the anniversary celebration," Ethan explained. His hazel eyes were fixed on Victoria.

"I suppose you want Victoria to handle the food."

Ethan nodded. "It's a done deal. She *will* cater the banquet dinner."

Quintin felt only partially relieved that Ethan and Victoria were discussing business. Why couldn't Victoria meet Ethan at his office? Why did he have to come to her home?

Victoria watched a myriad of expressions cross Quintin's face. His voice was strained, his manner stiff and formal. She wondered if his shoot had gone badly. Moving to his side, she slipped her hand in his. He squeezed her fingers.

Ethan, noticing the intimate gesture, reached up and buttoned the top button on his light-blue button-down shirt and tightened his navy-blue silk tie.

"I think it's about time I made it home. I still have a list of contributors to call before next week."

"How are the donations going?" Quintin asked him.

A slight frown creased his forehead. "Slow. But I'm sure they'll come in as promised. I've made calls to a few of my old Wall Street buddies to throw a few extra dollars this way for a good cause. They keep telling me I was a fool to give up the excitement of playing the market to beg for money for a not-for-profit operation, but there's no way I'd ever go back to that style of life."

Quintin gave him a warm, open smile for the first time. "Instead of making thousands of dollars a day in commissions from buying and selling stocks for wealthy people, you're now soliciting funds from them to keep your center's doors open."

Ethan nodded. "It sounds crazy, but at least I can sleep soundly at night knowing I'll never have to be tempted by those insider trading scams that might cost me not only a career but also my freedom." He walked over to Victoria and smiled down at her. "Thanks again."

Her right hand touched his shoulder in an affectionate gesture. "You're welcome, Ethan. I'll see you to the door."

Quintin waited in the dining room while Victoria escorted Ethan out of her apartment. He let out his breath in a ragged shudder. He had considered punching out his best friend because he found him alone with Victoria. Burying his face in his hands, he shook his head. What was the matter with him? He was losing it . . . he'd *lost* it.

He was feeling what he had felt the first time he met Victoria Jones; as if he were undergoing a midlife crisis. Then he had wanted a woman who was a stranger; but now Victoria Jones was no longer a stranger to him; he was her lover.

Lowering his hands, he stared at the patio doors across the living room. At first he wanted to get to know her, then he wanted to sleep with her, and now he wanted to marry her. For the first time in thirty-seven years he wanted a woman for a wife—his wife.

He had satisfied his craving for sailing with *Jamila,* and he had found companionship with Hannibal. Women—they were there when he *needed* them. And that was how he had viewed women in the past—he needed them. But only now did he *want* a woman. He wanted Victoria because he loved her with his every fiber of emotion. It was only now that he had to examine his feelings. Feelings of confusion, possessiveness, jealousy, insecurity, and fear tortured him. He wanted Victoria every hour, every minute, and every second of the day.

Even his work was off. The results of the early-morning shoot revealed that after he'd developed the film in his darkroom. Alicia Sherwood, his favorite model, looked wooden and hideously stiff, and the subsequent call to the designer revealed his dissatisfaction with the modeling session.

The excitement he normally felt when photographing a subject was missing. It was that excitement with its accompanying rush of adrenaline that made him better than most commercial artists. He was a perfectionist, and his best was never good enough.

He managed a wry smile. He had a second chance to redeem himself. Abayomi Koffigoh had agreed to repeat the shoot.

He turned, his smile widening as Victoria walked gracefully into the dining room. She wore the same slip dress she had worn the morning he first made love to her. It revealed the silken skin of her shoulders, arms, neck, and back. It ended mid-calf, but failed to conceal the perfection of her legs.

Victoria returned Quintin's smile, moving into his outstretched arms. Tilting her head back, her gaze swept slowly over his face. "How was your day?" It was the same question she used to ask Richard when he returned home from his hectic Georgetown law practice.

Quintin brushed his lips over hers. "Horrific until now." He deepened the kiss, his tongue slipping between her parted lips.

She moaned sensually, and a shudder shook his body. His hands went to her head, fingers threading through her unbound hair. Victoria moaned again as his fingers massaged her scalp, sending chills up and down her body.

"Quintin," she murmured weakly against his searching mouth. "I have work to . . . to do," she managed to gasp.

"So do I," he shot back, swinging her up in his arms.

"I do," she insisted, moaning against his chest.

"I'll help you," he countered, taking the stairs to her bedroom two at a time.

Pressing her lips to his hot throat, Victoria closed her eyes. "You can't cook," she whispered.

Those were the last three words she uttered until he had stripped the dress from her body, undressed himself, and positioned his naked body over hers, trembling uncontrollably. The corded muscles in his arms, the wild, glazed look in his eyes frightened and excited her at the same time.

"Oh," she muttered as he entered her in a smooth, strong thrusting motion of his hips.

Once sheathed in her moist heat, Quintin felt a rush of reason clear away the fog clouding his mind. He was back in control. The image of the first time he had made love to her swept over him, and he relived their erotic coupling in her shower stall.

Savoring the oneness, his hands framed her face and he placed gentle kisses on her closed eyelids. "I love you, darling," he crooned reverently. Her eyes opened and she stared back at him. "Please don't leave me." His fear of losing her had surfaced.

A slight frown made vertical slashes between her eyes. "What are you talking about, Quintin?"

Lowering his head, he buried his face between her neck and shoulder, inhaling the familiar fragrance of her perfume. The scent was Victoria: soft, sweet, hypnotic, and feminine.

"I've never craved a woman the way I crave you," he began quietly. "It's frightening, Vicky. You're not like an inanimate object that can be replaced when it wears out or is used up. You're a human being. You feel and react to people and situations."

"What are you trying to say?" she asked after a moment of silence.

"What I'm trying to say is that I'm afraid of doing or saying something that will cause you to send me away."

Her frown deepened. "I still don't know what you're talking about."

"Ethan."

"What about Ethan?"

Raising his head, Quintin caught her startled look. "I wanted to hit him," he confessed.

Her gaze widened. "For what?"

"For being here with you."

Victoria swallowed several times, trying to form the words rendering her speechless. "You . . . you think I'm—"

"I'm jealous, Vicky," he interrupted. "I know I have no right to be, but I'm jealous of every man who talks to you. I even thought that your friend Jo was a Joe. A Joseph kind of Joe."

She wanted to laugh, but didn't. Quintin's expression was one of pain. Her fingers touched his mouth. "Get a grip, darling. I'm with *you* and not some other man."

He lowered his head again. "I know," he mumbled. "But even if you decide to see someone else, remember he'll never love you the way I love you."

Her arms tightened around his neck, holding him close. "I love you, Quintin. I love you the way I've never loved any man." It was the truth. Though she had been infatuated with Richard, she knew she had never loved him. Not the way she loved the man she held to her heart.

"And I love you," he groaned, feeling the blood pool in his groin again as his flesh swelled for a second time within her.

He wanted to take her quickly, passionately, but he tempered his hunger, savoring the taste of her body as his mouth explored her throat, shoulders, and the firmness of her small breasts.

Quintin was always amazed how quickly her nipples hardened against his tongue and tightened between his teeth.

Making love to Victoria was exciting and as essential to him as eating and breathing. Each time he shared her body he thought of it as an honor and a privilege.

Victoria, eyes closed, gave in to the feel of Quintin filling every available inch of her body. His weight, hardness, and fullness evoked spasms of unbelievable pleasure that raced throughout her with no place to escape.

Her breath came quickly, rendering her helpless as the shudders of excitement swept her from head to toe. She felt heat, then chills at the base of her spine, between her legs, in her breasts, and in her head.

I'm going to go crazy. The litany began in the back of her brain, spinning faster and faster until she felt as if she *would* go crazy if Quintin didn't bring her to the pinnacle of fulfillment.

His movements quickened and both of them were out of control. She screamed blatant sexual demands and he complied, doing what she had pleaded with him to do. Holding nothing back, Quintin ground his hips to hers, allowing her to feel his strength, his hardness and the strong, pulsating length of his maleness as he drove into her yielding flesh over and over.

Without warning, her name was torn from the back of his throat and his movements quickened until his cries were joined by hers in a duet of unrestrained ecstasy.

Quintin withdrew and slid down the length of her moist, heaving body and buried his face between her trembling thighs and gently drank from her flowing well of feminine delight. Her shock was boundless as he renewed her desire and she soared and exploded again and again as his tongue caught the nectar of her musky sweetness.

Spent, sated, and exhausted, she fell asleep with Quintin lying between her thighs, his arms around her legs, holding her possessively.

Quintin lay motionless, unable to believe what he had just shared with Victoria. The beautiful witch made him do things to her he had never done with any other woman. She had woven a spell over him that made him helpless to resist her. He had fallen in love with her and would love her forever, and he knew he couldn't wait to ask her to marry him. He had to have her as his wife before the end of the year!

Twenty-one

"Are you certain you're all right?" Lydia asked Victoria for the second time that morning. She watched her move more slowly than usual and yawn incessantly.

"I'm just a little tired," Victoria confessed. She didn't want to tell Lydia that she and her brother had spent most of the night making love.

She gave Lydia a tired smile. "Check the computer and see how many cans of cherry filling we have on hand."

Lydia went over to a corner of the kitchen that had been set up as an office. She had learned quickly that every can, box, or sack of food in Victoria Jones's kitchen was inventoried on labeled disks. At any given moment Victoria would know if she had enough of any ingredient on hand to prepare whatever was requested by a client.

"You have one sixty-four-ounce can left," Lydia called out.

"That's enough for four pies," Victoria said. "Add cherry pie filling to the list." Cherry pie was Christine's parents' favorite pie and Nat had insisted she make enough for the invited guests and one for the honored couple.

Taking the last can of pie filling from the pantry, she opened it and poured the contents into a large aluminum bowl. Lydia rejoined her at the cooking island, watching as she ground whole nutmegs and added them to the filling.

"Nutmeg enhances the flavor," she explained to a rapt Lydia.

"Are you going to make lattice-tops or two-crust pies?"

"A lattice-top is visually more attractive. I'm going to show you how I make my pie crust so it's thin and flaky while still holding the filling."

Lydia, daring not to divert her gaze, watched as Victoria measured sifted flour into a bowl, added a pinch of salt, vegetable shortening, and butter.

"The butter gives the crust added richness." She blended the shortening and butter with a pastry blender until the mixture was crumbly, then sprinkled cold water over the mixture a tablespoon at a time until the pastry mix held together leaving the sides of the bowl clean. Lydia counted every spoonful of water.

Flouring the marble countertop, Victoria then divided the large ball into four and rolled out each ball until it was smooth and thin. She laid the rolling pin across the center of each pastry circle, gently folding half of it over the pin before transferring them to the pie pans.

Lydia was given the task of cutting pastry strips and weaving them evenly across the tops of the filled pie pans. She accomplished it so easily and quickly, Victoria felt secure enough for her to mix and roll out crusts for the apple and pecan pies Nat and Christine had also requested.

The two women worked throughout the morning and afternoon, preparing and freezing pies, trays of potato salad, cutting and marinating vegetable dishes, putting up batches of dough for breads and rolls, cutting out, baking, and decorating butter cookies.

"Tomorrow we prepare the meats and bake the cake," Victoria informed an exhausted Lydia as they both lay on lounge chairs on the patio.

"If I survive," Lydia moaned, closing her eyes.

"Are you ready to quit?"

Lydia sat up quickly. "Oh, no. It's just that I can't remember standing on my feet so many hours at a stretch."

"Running your own catering business is not easy. You have to prepare everything," Victoria explained. "When you work in a kitchen with other chefs you'll have a specialty. The chef at the sauté station will only concern himself with sautéed items, as well as the sauces and side dishes that appear on the same plate. The chef who oversees the pasta station is responsible for all pastas and accompanying sauces, as well as potatoes. If you decide to become a pastry chef you'll also have assistants, and your responsibility will be all desserts and some breads."

"What did you like best, Victoria?"

A slight smile softened her mouth. "Being the executive chef. I liked devising the menus and recipes. In other words, I determined the food's personality."

"I only hope I'll be half as good as you."

"You'll be better," Victoria stated honestly. "You have a natural bent for cooking. I sort of backed into it."

Lydia shifted, leaning on one elbow. "You didn't plan to become a chef?"

"I was trained to be a dancer," Victoria revealed. "I decided to go into the culinary arts when I broke my ankle. I didn't like cooking as much as I enjoyed seeing the presentation. I believe food should not only taste good but look tempting."

Lydia nodded, remembering the lunch Victoria had fixed for them: curried chicken balls on lettuce leaves, prosciutto-wrapped asparagus, Brie on stone wheat crackers, and fresh blueberries in cream.

"Would you rather prepare for buffet dining or a sit-down dinner?"

"Buffet dining. The presentation can be much more attractive and the variety of dishes appeals to a lot more people. With a sit-down dinner there's only a choice of the usual prime rib, chicken, or fish. With Saturday's celebration there will be everything from fresh and smoked ham to roast turkey, potato salad, mixed greens, fried okra, shrimp with blackeyed peas, deviled eggs. The list goes on and on. There's usually less waste with a buffet. If I prepare just one tray of let's say fried okra and it goes quickly, then everyone will move on to something else."

"What kind of cake are you going to make?" Lydia question.

"A double chocolate wedding cake."

"Double chocolate?"

"White chocolate and milk chocolate pound cake," Victoria explained. "When the layers are cut, both white and milk chocolate pound cake are revealed."

"That sounds incredible." Both women turned to see Quintin stepping over the wrought-iron railing. "Can I have a few samples?"

"This is called stepping over and entering instead of breaking and entering," Victoria teased, smiling up at Quintin.

Leaning over, he brushed a kiss on her lips, then moved over to Lydia and kissed her cheek. "How's it going, squirt?"

"I can make a pie crust like Victoria's," she said proudly.

Cocking his head, Quintin smiled at his sister. "You have the best for a teacher."

"She's incredible," Lydia said, her voice rising in excitement. "I'll be able to open my own restaurant right after I graduate. Daddy said he'll give me the money to set everything up."

"I suggest you try saving some of your own earnings," her brother suggested. "You appreciate things a lot more when you make a personal investment."

Lydia rose to her feet, shaking her head. "You sound like Mama."

"That's because she said the same thing to me when I was your age."

"And you'll probably say the same thing to your children."

Quintin smiled, his gaze shifting to Victoria. He missed the flicker of pain that crossed her face when Lydia mentioned children. He probably would say the same thing to the children he hoped to have with her.

"I hope I do," he said quietly.

"You hope you say the same thing or you hope you have children?" Lydia asked.

His gaze was fixed on Victoria. "Both."

It was all Victoria could do not to scream that she would never have his children. Her smile was forced as she stood up. "How did we go from food to babies?"

"I don't know, but I'm going home where I'm going to soak in a hot tub for an hour," Lydia said. "Whoever said cooking for a living is easy is a bald-faced liar."

"Thinking about quitting?" Victoria and Quintin chorused in unison.

Lydia flashed a sassy smile. "Never!" Turning, she went back into the living room. "See you tomorrow," she called out over her shoulder.

Quintin took the lounge chair she had just vacated, closing his eyes. "How was your day?"

"Tiring. And there's more tomorrow."

"Is there anything I can help you with?"

Victoria stared at his profile. "Yes, there is."

"Ask away, Vicky."

"Could you please sleep in your own bed tonight—alone."

He sat up, blinking at her as if he had never seen her before. "Why?"

"Because I'm bone-tired, Quintin. I can't spend the night wrestling with you, then spend eight hours on my feet without feeling fatigued. I've waited a long time to set up my own business not to want to do well."

A muscle throbbed noticeably in his jaw. She had called their lovemaking wrestling. Was that all it was to her—wrestling? Offering him her body meant that little to her.

"Are you saying that I'm ruining your business?"

"I'm not saying that, but . . ."

"Then what the hell *are* you saying, Vicky? Spit it out! You're an intelligent woman who never has a problem saying what you mean."

Her temper rose to meet his and she sprang to her feet. "Go away, Quintin, and leave me alone!"

He recoiled as if she had struck him. His body was rigid and his eyes widened in shock. She was sending him away. The fear he verbalized the night before had become a reality.

She didn't wait for him to step over the railing separating the two apartments as she turned and walked back to her place, closing the patio doors.

The soft click of the lock severed his trance, but it was another full minute before he reacted and made his way back to his own patio. He sat down on a chair, staring out into nothingness until the sun set, the sky darkened, and a red haze around the moon indicated a threat of rain for the next day. He ceased to think and feel, unable to believe what had happened.

Victoria stood under the spray of the shower, sobbing. It was the only place she could hide without Quintin hearing her from the neighboring apartment.

He wanted children. He wanted a baby and she couldn't give him a baby.

Sitting on the tiled floor of the stall, she cried until her sobs turned to whimpers, then to halting hiccuping sounds. She was drained.

The water turned cool, then cold, and her teeth began to chatter uncontrollably. Somewhere, somehow, she found the strength to rise from the floor and turn off the water.

She couldn't stop her teeth from clicking as she made her way out of the bathroom and into the bedroom, and without bothering to dry her body she lay across the bed and fell asleep.

The next morning she awoke, eyes swollen, her throat raw, and her limbs chilled from the air-conditioning. Glancing at the clock, she knew she only had an hour before Lydia arrived.

Reversing her daily ritual, Victoria soaked in a tub of hot water, swallowed a couple of aspirins with a glass of orange juice, then followed it with a cup of strong tea.

Lydia's expression registered shock when she noticed Victoria's puffy eyes and drawn cheeks but kept her silence. She didn't have to be as wise as Etta Mae Lord to know something had occurred between Victoria and Quintin.

Victoria was her employer and she knew she couldn't overstep the thin line that separated business from personal. But not so with Quintin. He was her brother and she loved him fiercely. She would discover what he had said or done to Victoria to bring about the pain she unsuccessfully tried to conceal each time she glanced at her.

She liked Victoria; liked her enough to have her as a sister-in-law.

Twenty-two

Victoria experienced a ripple of excitement for the first time in two days as she maneuvered her minivan down the driveway to the rear of the large Washington, D.C., town house. She had not seen Quintin after their Thursday evening spat and the damp and rainy weather on Friday had not lifted her dark mood. But early Saturday morning the rain had stopped and the hot weather returned with a promise of clear skies and a brilliant summer sun.

Christine Jones met Victoria and Lydia as they began unloading trays of food from the van. A nervous tic tortured the woman's left eye.

"Calm down, Christine," Victoria said softly. "We have everything under control."

Christine hugged Victoria and kissed her cheek. "I hope everything turns out okay. Believe it or not, my parents know nothing about this."

Victoria hugged her back. "Then it should be a wonderful surprise. This is my assistant Lydia Lord."

Lydia, smiling proudly, extended her hand. "Hello, Mrs. Jones."

Christine shifted her eyebrows, taking the proffered hand. "Please call me Christine. Nat's mother is Mrs. Jones."

"Where do you want us to set up, Christine?" Victoria questioned.

"Outside. Nat had the patio cleaned early this morning before the tables and chairs were delivered."

Victoria nodded. "I'm expecting two waiters from a local agency. When they arrive please send them to me."

"Will the four of you be enough to serve sixty-five people?" Christine asked.

"More than enough. Remember you have your own bartender, so I'll carve meats, Lydia will serve cold food, one waiter will serve hot food, and the extra person will float."

"You're the expert. I won't interfere."

"Can I sample the goods?" Nat Jones asked, coming out of the house and grinning broadly at his sister. He folded Victoria in a bear-hugging embrace, lifting her off her feet.

She kissed him on the mouth. "Why do you guys want samples all the time?" She thought of Quintin always wanting to sample what she had prepared. The thought swept the joy from her face.

"Because we're guys," he rationalized, easing her back to the ground.

She caught Lydia's hand, pulling her forward. "This is my assistant, Lydia Lord."

Lydia's mouth dropped slightly. "Aren't you Nathaniel Jones from the cable news channel?"

High color suffused Nat's sculpted golden-brown cheekbones as he stared at Lydia. He was never completely at ease with his celebrity status away from the television station. "Yes," he finally admitted.

"May I have your autograph, Mr. Jones?"

Nat winked at Lydia, whispering, "Later."

The offer surprised Victoria. Her brother always kept his professional life separate from his personal life. He was secure enough never to let them overlap.

The two waiters arrived, assisting Victoria and Lydia as they unloaded the van and set up the Sterno heaters under the trays of hot foods.

Victoria personally supervised the unloading of the cake. It was baked in four separate layers and decorated with white chocolate butter frosting. She had used a large decorating bag, utilizing five metal tips to make the curls and pipe the grapevine and flower designs. White chocolate curls and shavings would grace the third and top layers.

More than a dozen round tables, each seating six, with attached umbrellas, were positioned around the Joneses' large backyard. The area for serving food and beverages was also shaded by a tent.

By one o'clock the first guests began arriving, and Christine had calmed down enough to become the gracious hostess.

The two waiters greeted the guests with trays of cold shrimp with an accompanying cocktail sauce, deviled eggs, mushrooms stuffed with crabmeat or smoked ham and seasoned bread crumbs, crab puffs, chow-chow, a variety of cheeses and crackers, and a spicy guacamole.

William and Marion Jones arrived with their usual flair, Marion declaring the food looked too good to eat.

She made a big show of kissing and hugging Victoria. "Sweetheart, you've outdone yourself," she gushed.

"Thank you, Mom." Turning to Lydia, she introduced her to her mother as her assistant.

Marion curved an arm around Victoria's waist. "Now, you listen to what all my daughter teaches you, and one day you'll be quite good."

"That is my intention, Mrs. Jones."

Marion gave her a warm smile, nodding, then turned to Victoria. "Sweetheart, I wanted to let you know that your father and I are giving a little something at our house for the head of the Togolese Union for Democracy two weeks from today. Perhaps you remember him. Mr. Kodjo was the former secretary-general of the Organization of African Unity."

"I remember him well."

"Well, he's agreed to come and he's bringing his nephew Yaovi. You do remember the very handsome young man who studied economics and international law at Oxford. He was always very interested in you."

How well she remembered Yaovi—she and every other woman on the African continent. Yaovi was spectacularly handsome. He claimed the most sensual eyes and mouth of any man Victoria had ever seen.

"How can I forget him," she said with a mysterious smile.

"I'm not trying to play matchmaker, sweetheart, but I just wanted to let you know in case you decide to come without an escort."

"I suppose your 'little something' will be a formal dinner?"

"Of course, sweetheart."

"I'll be there, Mom."

"With an escort?"

Closing her eyes briefly, she thought of Quintin. How she wished she could bring him with her, but she knew that was not possible. The break had been quick and bloodless. There was no way she wanted to reopen the wound.

"Without an escort," she finally said. "Let Yaovi know that I'm looking forward to seeing him again."

Marion clasped her delicate hands together, smiling. "Wonderful. Now, Lydia, please serve me some of Victoria's wonderful potato salad."

Lydia spooned a helping of potato salad onto Marion Jones's plate, frowning. She had overheard the conversation between Victoria and her mother. She had also noted the expression on Victoria's face when her mother had spoken of the man named Yaovi. She had to let Mrs. Jones know that her daughter wasn't interested in this Yaovi because she was in love with her brother.

Lydia knew she had to act and act quickly.

* * *

Victoria tipped the two waiters, thanking them for their help. Both of them requested that she ask for them again whenever she catered another event in the D.C. area. She promised she would. The two young men were Howard University students and supplemented their meager incomes by waiting tables and serving parties.

Sitting in the van beside Lydia, Victoria smiled at her. "Well, do you still want to be a chef?"

Lydia nodded, smiling a tired smile. "More than ever before. Even though you prepared all the food, I felt a personal satisfaction seeing everyone eat. I can't believe there weren't any leftovers."

She had to agree. The invited guests had come with prodigious appetites, devouring every morsel of food in sight. If she hadn't removed the top layer of the cake for the honored couple their guests would have eaten that, too.

"It was a success," she said softly.

"The first of many successes," Lydia replied.

Both women were quiet on the return drive to Baltimore. Victoria refused Lydia's offer to help unload the van, saying she would unload it the next day. She slipped several large bills into the younger woman's hand as she sat in her tiny Honda CRX.

"It's a tip," she said before Lydia opened her mouth to protest. "Thanks for your help."

Lydia stared at the money. "I should be the one thanking you. I should pay you instead of you paying me."

"Maybe one day you will pay me."

A sly grin teased Lydia's mouth upward. "Maybe I will."

Victoria watched the red taillights from the car as it pulled away from the curb, then turned and retreated to her own apartment. She was past being exhausted, and she knew the exhaustion wasn't just from not getting enough sleep or from standing on her feet for hours.

The fatigue was emotional. She had soared to great heights with Quintin. It was only when she fell that she realized the enormity of their separation.

She had looked forward to seeing him, hearing his voice, and having him hold her to his body. He lived only a few feet from her yet she felt as if they were separated by miles.

She loved him—loved him with an intensity she had never felt for another man; and she knew she would never love another man the way she loved him.

Since her divorce she'd been sure she never wanted to remarry. But she'd found herself thinking of marriage again. Thinking that this time it would be different. She could have a career that her husband respected; and he would be willing to share in her successes as well as her failures.

He would want her for herself and not for the children he hoped she would give him to carry on his name and his genes.

Not the child Richard wanted to nurture and mold into what he had failed to become.

The child Richard wanted that would be an object of vanity—a miniature clone of him.

Her steps were slow and heavy as she made her way up the stairs to the front door. The pounding rhythms hit her the moment she stepped into the hallway. Quintin was playing his music full tilt.

Victoria didn't know how it happened, but she alternated pounding on his door with her fist while ringing his doorbell.

The door swung open, and she stared up at a bearded Quintin. His gold-brown gaze swept quickly over her, missing nothing. "What?"

She registered the sharpness in his bored tone, but refused to back down. "Turn it down."

He shifted an eyebrow and yawned. "Good night, Miss Jones."

"I'll call the police," she threatened.

"Good."

Turning away, she opened the door to her apartment and slammed it as hard as she could. Pressing her back against the door, she bit down hard on her lower lip. She was torturing herself. Just seeing him again was torture, so she decided the best way to get over Quintin Lord was not to see him again.

But that didn't prove as easy as she thought it would be. Her nights were filled with images of him and their passionate lovemaking. The images were so real that she awoke in a sweat, her heart pounding and her body throbbing.

Victoria sat across from Joanna in a D.C. restaurant, drinking from a glass of iced tea. The mysterious smile on Jo's face revealed more than what the redhead was saying.

"So, Ethan has hired you to plan the center's fifth anniversary celebration?" Victoria repeated the news her friend just revealed.

"Isn't that a gas?"

"He or the idea?"

Jo blushed furiously. "Both," she admitted with a sigh. "Victoria . . . Victoria . . ."

"That is my name," she teased.

"Well . . . well, it goes a little farther than business."

Victoria decided not to make it easy for Jo. "Are you saying you and Ethan are involved?"

Her flush deepened. "Well—not really. We've had dinner a few times."

"Dinner at his place?" Jo nodded. "Well, the man happens to be a wonderful cook."

"It's not only his cooking, Victoria. It's Ethan."

"What's wrong with him?"

"Nothing. He's perfect. As perfect as a man can get, I suppose." Jo's gaze was fixed somewhere over Victoria's head. "I don't know how to say this."

Leaning over, Victoria grasped Jo's hands, holding them firmly. "Are you trying to say that he's not into women?"

"Oh, no! No never." She pulled her hands free.

"What is it?"

"He's somewhat shy. He has the most exquisite manners, and he does all of the right things, but he hasn't . . ."

Victoria threw back her head and laughed. "He hasn't tried to get you into bed," she finished perceptively.

Jo nodded again. "I hope it's not me."

"It's not you, Jo. It's the man. You're so used to the slobs who take you out to dinner, then expect you to be their dessert that you don't recognize a real man when you finally meet one. Did you notice the furnishings in his house? They're heirloom pieces. And we both know he didn't pick up that Rodin sculpture sitting in his living room at a thrift shop. Even without seeing Ethan's portfolio you know he's anything but ordinary."

"I don't want to get hurt, Vicky."

"You won't if you don't give him your heart." *Unlike me with Quintin,* she thought.

"You're right. I've thought myself in love so many times that this is all new to me."

"He may be preoccupied because he's waiting for Ryan's adoption to go through. Just let Ethan establish where he wants the relationship to go."

Jo shrugged her shoulders. "You do know that Quintin is going to be Ryan's godfather once the adoption is final."

"No, I didn't," she answered truthfully.

Jo gave Victoria a long, penetrating look. "Aren't you seeing Quintin?"

"Why do you think I'm seeing him?"

"Because I know what I observed the day we went sailing, Vicky. I saw the man with his tongue down your throat." She ignored Victoria's slight gasp. "And I know that he hasn't been the nicest person to be around lately."

Victoria slumped against the padded back on her chair, frowning at Joanna. "So this little dinner date is not about Ethan, but about Quintin and me. Did Ethan tell you to discuss Quintin with me?"

Jo nodded, biting down on her lower lip. "I wanted to talk to you about *Ethan,* and when I mentioned I was going to see you for dinner he suggested I ask you about Quintin."

She felt some of her tension ease. "Thank you for not lying, Jo."

Leaning forward on her seat, Jo asked, "What happened between the two of you?"

"I haven't seen him for a week."

"Why?"

"Because I can't ever give him what he'd like to have."

A frown creased Jo's forehead. "What is that?" she asked quietly.

She exhaled, her eyes darkening with pain. "A child."

The natural color faded from Jo's face, leaving a liberal sprinkling of freckles. "You're kidding, aren't you?"

"No." Victoria shook her head for emphasis. "I had an accident ten years ago, a very serious accident, and after I woke up in the recovery room I was told that I'd never have children. My husband left me because I couldn't give him a child." Her expression hardened. "I don't intend for another man to do that to me again."

"But the two of you could've adopted a child."

"Richard wanted his own children. His exact words were, he didn't want 'someone else's throwaways'."

"He sounds like a horse's ass," Jo snapped, her eyes shooting sparks of copper fire.

She couldn't help smiling. "Don't tell anyone, but he is."

Both women dissolved in a paroxysm of laughter, lifting

the dark mood. Jo signaled their waiter and ordered two glasses of white wine.

Victoria took a sip of her wine, then leaned over the table. "What has Quintin done to make Ethan solicit you to be his envoy on this mission of peace?"

"It's more like a mission of mercy. I'm here to save the children. Quintin volunteered to help with the stage sets for the big production number and apparently he got into a confrontation with one of the older boys. He complained to Ethan that he wasn't going to take anyone 'getting up in his grill,' and the next time Quintin tried it the two of them would settle it outside—in the back."

"Grill?"

"His face, Vicky. Ethan had to translate the term to me, too."

"How did Ethan handle the situation?"

"He talked to the kid for a long time and finally got him to calm down. He was less successful with Quintin. He hasn't seen Quintin nor has he returned his phone calls since last Saturday."

"That was the last time I saw him, too. He was playing his music loud enough to wake the dead and when I threatened to call the police he called my bluff."

"Did you call them?"

"No. But he did turn it down ten minutes later."

There was a long pause before Jo spoke again. "What are you doing to do, Vicky?"

"Go on with my life as if Quintin Lord never existed."

Frowning slightly, Jo stared at Victoria, giving her a look that said she didn't believe her. "Are you sure?"

Victoria blinked slowly, nodding. "Very sure." And at that moment she was.

Twenty-three

Victoria considered talking to Quintin about bullying young kids, but each time she approached his door she turned around and reentered her own apartment.

She remembered his confession that he wanted to punch Ethan when he discovered him in her apartment. She found it difficult to associate Quintin with violence. It seemed so out of character for him especially when she recalled his gentleness and tender lovemaking.

The dilemma was solved for her. As she sat out on her patio she heard the doors of his apartment slide open. Sitting in the darkness, she blended into the shadowy night.

"Quintin." Her soft voice carrIed easily in the stillness. She heard his sharp intake of breath and smiled. He didn't answer her, and she continued. "There's a nasty rumor going around about you threatening to take someone out in the parking lot behind the cultural center. Don't you think you're a little old to be brawling like a thug? And especially with a kid."

"Are you willing to take the kid's place, Miss Jones?"

"Of course not. I've never brawled like a common—"

"What came out of *his* mouth was common, Miss Jones," he said, interrupting her. "For your information I merely warned him about using foul language in front of the girls, and he said something about his First Amendment right to free speech. I merely gave him a choice: clean up his mouth or he was off the project."

She felt her face burn in embarrassment and she was grateful for the cover of darkness. "I'm sorry, Quintin. I suppose I only heard half of the story."

There was only the sound of chirping crickets and the occasional slapping sound of tires from a passing vehicle before Quintin spoke again. "Apology accepted."

A slight smile lifted his mouth. He couldn't see Victoria, but his nostrils had detected the scent of her perfume. She was so close yet so far away.

The past week had been hell. He wanted to go to her and hold her, to kiss away the bitter words they had traded. He wanted her and he needed her. But more than that, he loved her. He'd never stop loving her.

When Lydia had called him and read him the riot act, he retaliated by hanging up on her. He then retreated into a world of silence, not answering his phone or returning calls.

He was hurting, he was bleeding, and the woman who could stem the flow was sitting less than twenty feet away. She could heal him, could make him whole.

"Good night, Quintin."

Her quiet voice floated toward him, and he held on to the sides of his chair to keep from going to her. "Good night, Victoria."

He registered the soft click of her door, then he did what he had been doing for a week: he sat out in the darkness until the sky lightened.

Victoria received an unexpected call from her sister the morning of their parents' dinner.

"Why don't I pick you up and we'll drive down to D.C. together," Kimberly Abernathy suggested.

"Wouldn't it be better if I pick you up, Kimm? After all, you're closer to D.C. than I am."

"I'm already in Baltimore. I'm leaving the baby with Russell's mother."

"How is she going to feed him?"

Kimberly laughed. "I'll pump enough milk to last him until I get back. I've got my figure back and I'm ready to do some serious partying."

"What time should I expect you?"

"How about three?"

Victoria glanced at the clock on the bedside table. "Make it four. I have an appointment to have my hair done at eleven."

"Four it is. I'll see you then."

She hung up, staring at the dress she had planned to wear to the dinner party. It was an exquisite evening ensemble with vertical bands of dark sapphire, blue velvet, and black silk chiffon with long sleeves, a fitted bodice, a velvet neckband. The full, gored skirt was made for dancing. The vertical bands, ending at the waistline, covered her breasts and her breastbone. The body suit she had purchased to match her own skin tone provided a modicum of modesty. Three inches of silk heels in a sapphire blue completed the outfit.

Like Kimm, she was also ready to do some serious partying. But unlike Kimm she was free to flirt with whomever she pleased. Perhaps if she flirted enough she would be able to forget about her neighbor.

Victoria stared at her reflection in the mirror on the dressing table. The soft light in the bedroom where she had grown up was flattering to her expertly made-up face. Her hair had been cut close to her scalp and curled into a cap of loose ringlets. The haircut made her eyes appear larger, and the overall effect made her look younger than her thirty-one years.

The cocktail hour was to begin promptly at seven, leaving her less than ten minutes to dress. She slipped into her dress and pulled up the zipper, artfully concealed in one of the velvet bands in the back. She stepped into her heels, then fastened a pair of sapphire-and-diamond earrings which had belonged to her great-grandmother in her pierced lobes.

A babble of voices, male and female, American and foreign, drifted up from the living room as she made her way down the carpeted curving staircase in the Joneses' magnificent Georgian-style home.

She caught a glimpse of colorful African prints along with the traditional tuxedo. She had grown up watching her father attend and preside over formal dinners for many African dignitaries in the thirty years he had worked for the State Department.

She spotted Yaovi immediately. He towered over most of the men in the room. She also recognized the cut of his suit. Yaovi had always favored his Armani suits over the traditional African garb.

Unusually large dark eyes followed her progress across the room as yards of black-and-sapphire chiffon floated out around her legs. A full, sensual mouth smiled, revealing perfect white teeth.

Yaovi excused himself and met Victoria halfway across the room. He grasped her hands, kissing her fingers. "What a vision," he crooned, lowering his head in a slight bow. "Victoria, you are more beautiful than I remembered."

The burgundy lip color on her mouth shimmered as she pursed her lips. "Yaovi—always the charmer."

He released one of her hands and pressed his left one to his heart. "You wound me, Victoria. You know I'd wait a lifetime for you. The last time we met you were taken."

She tilted her chin, drowning in his obsidian gaze. "And how many wives do you have now?"

He managed to look insulted. "I have not taken a wife."

"What are you waiting for?" She knew Yaovi to be at least thirty-five.

"You." The word rolled smoothly off his silken tongue.

"I'm afraid you'll have to wait forever because the lady happens not to be available."

Victoria froze, and if Yaovi hadn't been holding her hand she was certain she would've fallen. Turning slowly, she stared up at Quintin Lord.

"What are you doing here?" she whispered.

Quintin reached out and extracted her hand from Yaovi's. "Thanks, buddy, for watching over Victoria. I'll take over now."

Yaovi stood speechless. He managed to nod as he watched the man lead Victoria Jones away. His shock was temporary, for within seconds a woman strolled over, draping her bare arm over the fabric of his expertly tailored suit jacket. Smiling, he lowered his head to listen to her quiet voice. His deep laugh floated over the woman's ear and she winked knowingly up at him. He reached for a glass of champagne from a passing waiter, handed it to her, then claimed a glass for himself.

Victoria pulled against Quintin's strong grip, but she knew she couldn't free herself without making a scene. Especially not in front of her parents or their guests.

Her stunned gaze swept over Quintin, taking in the single-button black tuxedo jacket, silk banded-collar, white shirt, black dress trousers, black patent-leather dress slippers, and the single diamond stud in his left ear. He had traded his gold hoops for the brilliant tiny diamond.

"To answer your question as to why I'm here . . ." He took a glass of champagne from a waiter, gave it to her, and, without releasing her hand, took one for himself.

"Yes," he continued, "why I'm here. I received a rather

cryptic message on my telephone answering machine saying that if I didn't want to lose the woman I loved to a magnificent, British-accented, English-speaking African gentleman who travels to Milan once a year to replenish his wardrobe, then I'd better show up here at seven tonight. And it appears that I arrived just in time, Vicky."

"You can't be talking about Yaovi?"

"Was the man drooling over your hand Yoda?"

"Yaovi, Quintin," she corrected.

"Whatever," he drawled. "Now, drink your champagne and act nice, darling. Then we'll disappear for a few minutes and talk."

She tried pulling away from him. He had no right to barge into her parents' home and embarrass her. "Let me go, Quintin."

He tightened his grip, his lips curling under his silky mustache. "Please, Vicky, don't make me act common in front of your parents and their esteemed guests."

"You *are* common to come barging in here," she retorted.

Quintin took a sip of champagne, his gaze fixed on her beautiful, delicate face. "Must I remind you that I was invited. How else would I have found you. Drink your champagne, love. It happens to be an excellent vintage."

She took a sip from the fluted glass, feeling the heat flood her face and neck as she watched everyone in the room staring at her and Quintin.

"Come with me," she ordered, leading him in the direction of her father's library. He preceded her inside the large room and she closed the door behind them.

Turning to face him, Victoria found she couldn't keep her hunger for him from showing. Even though she knew it was wrong to be alone with him, at that moment she was helpless to resist the tall man standing less than three away. He had affected his own style of formal dress, and the overall effect was devastatingly appealing. The collarless shirt, the absence of a tie, and the earring said Quintin Jones was his own person; a person who would throw convention to the wind if there was a cause he truly believed in.

He glanced around the library, quickly assessing the photographs lining the wall. His gaze lingered on the portraits of distinguished men dressed in the height of fashion from the mid- to late-1800s.

Turning back to Victoria, Quintin held out a hand, taking her glass and putting it down on a polished mahogany side table with his. "Please sit down, Vicky."

She grasped his hand and permitted him to seat her in a brocade armchair. He took a matching one, facing her.

Crossing a leg over his knee, he stared at her. "Don't you have something to tell me?"

Victoria crossed her legs, too, allowing him a glimpse of silk sapphire-blue pumps from under the flowing yards of black-and-blue chiffon. "I don't know what you're talking about.

"Don't you?"

"Don't answer my question with a question, Quintin."

He continued to stare at her, unblinking. After a deafening silence, he lowered his gaze and laced his fingers together.

"Something is bothering you; something that goes a lot deeper than you trying to make a go of your catering business. I've also had time to think about your evasiveness whenever I asked you about your dance career. You're hiding something from me, and you're hiding from yourself."

Her eyes narrowed slightly. "You're wrong."

"Am I, Vicky? The only time you're not hiding is when we're in bed. Only when we make love do I get to know the real Victoria Jones. Then you hold nothing back. But outside of bed you're cautious, guarded, and sometimes distant." Leaning forward, he held both of her hands, not permitting her to escape. "Who did this to you?"

She looked at her hands cradled in his and smiled a sad smile. "No one did it to me, Quintin." Her voice was barely a whisper. "I did it to myself. I permitted someone to define who I was."

"Who was he?"

"My ex-husband."

"What happened, darling?"

Her head came up, and she met his intense gaze. "I told myself I wasn't a woman." She related details of her accident and Richard's subsequent reaction to her not being able to bear his children.

Quintin tightened his hold on her hands and pulled her fluidly from her chair and onto his lap. He cradled her gently to his chest and buried his face in her hair.

"He was a fool, Victoria," he finally said after her whispered words faded. "You're more woman than any woman I've ever known. The only thing I'll say is that I love you and that I want you as my wife."

"Quintin," she sobbed against his chest, "you still want me even if I can't give you a child?"

His hands searched under her chin, raising her face. He surveyed the unshed tears in her eyes. "Is that why you sent me away? Because you can't have children?"

She nodded, closing her eyes. She couldn't bear to see the look of revulsion on his face. Richard hadn't been able to conceal his when she told him that she would never bear a child.

Quintin's expression was taut before a look of amusement softened his mouth. His arms became bands of steel around her waist. "You little fool. Do you think I want you because I want children?" She nodded shyly. "Well, you're wrong, Miss Victoria Jones. Don't you think if I wanted children I would've had some before now?"

"But . . . but . . ."

He covered her mouth with his fingers, then replaced them with his mouth. He deepened the kiss as she twisted on his lap, her arms going around his neck.

"Quintin." His name came out in a sighing groan while his lips explored her eyelids, the curving slope of a cheekbone before finding her mouth again.

"You beautiful, silly witch. My loving you and wanting to marry you had nothing to do with children," he said softly against her ear. "If you decide you want a child we can always adopt. There's no shortage of black children looking for a home filled with love. And that's what we would have, Vicky, a home filled with love."

Pulling back, she smiled up at him. "And don't forget delicious food."

He returned her smile. "And a beautiful mother."

"And a wonderfully talented, handsome father."

"And a few neurotic pets," he added.

There was no way Victoria could conceal her joy as she melted against his chest, her head resting on his shoulder.

"When do you want to get married, Quintin?"

"How about next week?"

"That soon?"

He pressed a kiss to her hair. "You'd rather wait?"

Biting down on her lower lip, she thought about the agony of waiting. She shook her head, smiling. "No."

"Your place or mine?"

"For what?"

"Where do you want to live?"

Extracting herself from his embrace, Victoria stood up and began pacing, the flowing skirt of her dress floating out around her feet in a cloud of shimmering blue-black.

"I have to have my kitchen," she mused aloud.

Crossing his arms over his chest, Quintin studied the graceful outline of her body. "And I have to have my darkroom."

"But I also need my room to work out at the barre."

Rising to his feet, Quintin went to her and folded her against his body. "I guess you win. What we can do is knock down the wall separating the two apartments and join the lofts. Or we can keep the apartments for professional purposes and buy a little place somewhere in the country."

Tilting her face to his, she kissed his chin. "I kind of like being a neighbor."

Lowering his head, Quintin intoned, "Thou shalt not covet thy neighbor's house; thou shalt not covet thy neighbor's wife, nor his manservant, nor his maidservant, nor his ox, nor his ass, nor anything that is thy neighbor's."

She laughed. "I guess that means we'll have to buy a little place somewhere in the country."

"I thought you'd see it my way." He took a quick glance at his watch. "We still have time before dinner is served to let your folks know that we plan to get married."

"There is something I need to know before we go back."

"What is it?"

"Who called you and left the message on your machine?"

"Your mother," Quintin replied smugly.

A shock flew through her. "My mother? But how? She never met you."

"Lydia told her about us, and apparently the meddling little brat was determined to have you as a sister-in-law."

Victoria's mouth quirked with humor. "I knew there was something I liked about her right away."

"That's exactly how I felt about you the moment I saw you," Quintin confessed. "Especially since you were so willing to show me what I would get if I managed to get you to fall in love with me."

A frown wrinkled her brow. "What are you talking about?"

Quintin dropped a kiss on the end of her nose. "You

were sprawled on my living room floor wearing the tiniest pair of panties . . ."

Victoria stopped his words as her mouth covered his, molding her length to his. They were breathing heavily when they parted.

Arm-in-arm, they made their way to the living room, love shining from their eyes and joy filling their hearts, to announce their good news to the world.

Epilogue

Victoria opened the door, shivering slightly as the cool winter air swept into the room. The flames from a roaring fire leapt as the burning logs crackled loudly when sparks flew up in a shimmering red-gold display.

"Merry Christmas. Come on in."

Ethan, Joanna, and Ryan filed into the room, arms ladened with gaily wrapped packages.

"Merry Christmas to you, too," Ethan said, a wide smile on his handsome face.

"Welcome, welcome," Quintin greeted his guests. He handed Ryan a small, squirming puppy with a large red bow around its neck. "Merry Christmas, Ryan."

The young boy cradled the black ball of fur to his chest, his eyes filled with delight. "Thank you, Quintin."

"You're quite welcome," he told his godson. "Hannibal's very proud of this little guy, so make certain you take good care of him.

"I promise I will." The child's joy was boundless.

Quintin then took coats, hats, gloves, and scarves from the three while Victoria placed the packages under the sweeping branches of a live, decorated evergreen.

"Everything looks so nice," Jo remarked, taking in the furnishings in the Lord living room.

Ethan, walking to the fireplace, glanced up at the painting over the mantel. "When did you do this one?" he asked Quintin.

Quintin placed a hand on his friend's shoulder. "I did the sketch the night you came to ask me to be Ryan's godfather."

"It's magnificent." His hazel eyes studied the painting. "If you ever think of selling . . ."

"It's not for sale, buddy. It's a part of my private collection." There was another painting he had done of Victoria, but that one was not for public viewing. Victoria had agreed to sit for him after they had been married for a year. He considered the nude portrait his finest work, but he had kept his promise not to show it. It hung on a wall in their bedroom.

"I think it's time I commission you to do a family portrait," Ethan stated solemnly.

Quintin's teeth shone whitely under his mustache. "Do I hear what I think I'm hearing? You and Jo?"

Ethan nodded. "She's agreed to marry me. Ryan was overjoyed when I told him that she would be his mother."

"I'll do the portrait, and I'll give it to you as a wedding gift."

Ethan extended his hand. "Thanks, buddy."

Quintin shook the proffered hand. "You're welcome, buddy."

His gaze drifted over to Victoria as she sat on a love seat with Joanna, admiring her engagement ring. It had been a year and a half since his neighbor walked into his apartment wearing practically nothing under a robe while issuing a demand that he not play his music so loud.

Victoria glanced up and met his gaze, and a mysterious smile touched her sensual mouth. Pursing her lips, she winked at him.

He returned her knowing wink. Ethan had Ryan and Joanna, and they had each other.

But that would all change in the upcoming year. They'd

decided to adopt a child. There was more than enough love in their hearts for any child who would be fortunate enough to claim them as parents.

Dear Readers:

I would like to thank all of you for your wonderful response to my previous Arabesque releases—HAPPILY EVER AFTER and HIDEAWAY.

The response for HIDEAWAY was overwhelming, so when Matthew Sterling made his appearance in one pivotal scene in HIDEAWAY he demanded his own story. This mysterious man who lives by his own set of rules was granted his wish. Matt's novel will be released April, 1997.

And to answer hundreds of questions—*yes*—Joshua Kirkland will get his own story.

Whether I write stories about finding love and passion in a small town or across a continent, I want to give you the passion and sensuality you've come to expect in a romance novel. I hope I've achieved this with Victoria and Quintin in HOME SWEET HOME.

I welcome comments from readers who can write me at:

Rochelle Alers
P.O. Box 690
Freeport, New York 11520-0690

Please enclose SASE for reply. I look forward to hearing from you soon.

Rochelle Alers is a native New Yorker who now resides in a picturesque fishing village on Long Island where she draws inspiration to write her novels and short stories. Her interests include music, art, gourmet food, meditation, and traveling.